Siren Publishing

It Takes Special Forces

9

Love on the Rocks

Dixie Lynn Dwyer

It Takes Special Forces

Essie Salter is not just shy, she's scared, too. A victim of stalking, forced to disappear and start a new life in order to survive, she winds up in South Carolina. Her fear of soldiers is justified. But she's trying to learn to be confident and strong despite daily panic attacks and new insecurities.

However, it seems Special Forces can hinder her thought-out strategy of survival and remaining undetected. Especially since those forces come in the form of five very well-trained, attractive, and determined Special Forces soldiers. They infiltrate her heart and readjust her strategy, and just in the nick of time, as her stalker discovers her hiding place.

Her men have built up her self-confidence and given her the tools to survive, but it's her need to fight for her life—and for her lovers—that will be put to the test in a do-or-die situation.

Genre: Contemporary, Ménage a Trois/Quatre, Romantic Suspense
Length: 56,982 words

IT TAKES SPECIAL FORCES

Love on the Rocks 9

Dixie Lynn Dwyer

Siren Publishing, Inc.
www.SirenPublishing.com

DEDICATION

Dear readers,

Thank you for purchasing this legal copy of *It Takes Special Forces*.

Essie is living in fear and unable to trust anyone she meets. She has a secret and it takes a good friend and a special town to help her see that there are people she can trust.

She was a victim of a stalker, an obsessed military man willing to kill anyone in his path to find her.

Essie never expected to fall in love, and certainly not with five men. She learns to trust them, knows that they understand her anxiety and fears, and they help her regain her self-confidence and once again feel like she is living a normal life.

Love is a very powerful thing, indeed. A woman once scared of her own shadow, timid and shy, becomes empowered by the support of loving, empathetic men as well as some self-defense training. The love of her men makes Essie ready to give the ultimate sacrifice to protect them, just as they are willing to give their lives to protect her and save her from her stalker.

May you enjoy her story. Happy reading.

Hugs!
Dixie

ABOUT THE AUTHOR

People seem to be more interested in my name than where I get my ideas for my stories from. So I might as well share the story behind my name with all my readers.

My momma was born and raised in New Orleans. At the age of twenty, she met and fell in love with an Irishman named Patrick Riley Dwyer. Needless to say, the family was a bit taken aback by this as they hoped she would marry a family friend. It was a modern day arranged marriage kind of thing and my momma downright refused.

Being that my momma's families were descendants of the original English speaking Southerners, they wanted the family blood line to stay pure. They were wealthy and my father's family was poor.

Despite attempts by my grandpapa to make Patrick leave and destroy the love between them, my parents married. They recently celebrated their sixtieth wedding anniversary.

I am one of six children born to Patrick and Lynn Dwyer. I am a combination of both Irish and a true Southern belle. With a name like Dixie Lynn Dwyer it's no wonder why people are curious about my name.

Just as my parents had a love story of their own, I grew up intrigued by the lifestyles of others. My imagination as well as my need to stray from the straight and narrow made me into the woman I am today.

Enjoy *It Takes Special Forces* and allow your imagination to soar freely.

For all titles by Dixie Lynn Dwyer, please visit
www.bookstrand.com/dixie-lynn-dwyer

IT TAKES SPECIAL FORCES

Love on the Rocks 9

DIXIE LYNN DWYER

Prologue

Essie Salter walked down the side street of the city only a block from her apartment building. She was tired from a long day at work, her mind on having to go home and clean the apartment, and do grocery shopping tomorrow for the week. She exhaled. She was unorganized, frazzled, and wondered how she got to this point of monotony and routine. She always thought that living in the city would bring her excitement, some spice in her otherwise boring life, and entertainment. Well, the club scene, the bar scene, and the dining out with friends anyway.

Friday or Saturday evenings were becoming a bore. Her job was a hell of a lot better than if she took the one in the suburbs with Mr. Ranger, her dad's old friend, though. How boring that would have been, to be the office sales manager, and basically secretary, for that man? God, her life would have been shit. Instead, she took a chance and applied to Strober and King, a large company in the city that promoted and sold over a thousand products and services throughout the United States. She applied for a job in one particular department that was hiring. The boss was a hard-ass. She found out months after being there that he didn't get along with anyone, and his assistants didn't last long.

She shook her head as she rounded the corner. Gary Perk was just an obsessive, compulsive perfectionist. He rubbed off on her, and they got along well because she was an overachiever and she didn't want her parents to tell her "I told you so" if she failed. So, she sucked it up, took his bad attitude with a grain of salt, and eventually they got along perfectly. She had to smile. He was a great boss, and her job as product promoter and contract negotiator was awesome. Her ability to handle research and detail-oriented documents was a gift. She could do a wide range of jobs, but this one was consistent and the pay excellent. She was making it on her own. Twenty-four years old and things were only looking better.

Her fellow colleagues couldn't compete with her performance, and so Gary treated her with respect, and she was his number one employee. But, oh, what a process the last two years had been.

She felt proud, and just as the smile formed on her lips, and her heart filled with joy at her success here in the city, she felt the gloved hand go over her mouth, and a thick, large muscular arm go around her waist. Her entire body tightened up, and fear consumed her instantly. She reacted, squirming, pushing downward to get the man off of her. She tried screaming but couldn't with the thick glove over her mouth and nose. She could hardly breathe. The panicked feeling consumed her when this person in black pulled her into the side ally. *Oh God, I'm going to be raped and mugged. Oh God.*

She tried kicking and moving her arms and legs, but it was no use. This guy was so big and strong, and then she was shoved against the building, and the strikes came at her one after the next. She didn't have time to recover. A slam to her stomach and she lost her breath. She couldn't scream. Then a shot to her mouth, her head, her stomach again. He was using her as a punching bag. She scraped at his body but whatever he wore was like armor, hard, rough, and her nails couldn't penetrate through. He just kept grunting and striking her until she couldn't take the pain and begged for mercy, and then begged for death.

Essie shot up from bed, gasping, unable to breathe.

She clenched the sheets covering her, threw them back, and fell from the bed to her knees on the floor, her mind coming back to the present from the horrific nightmare. She reached for the crumpled paper bag on the bedside table, knocking over her cell phone and the box of tissues. Her throat was so tight she could barely breathe. The inhale, short and painful as she somehow gripped the bag in a fist, brought it to her mouth, and started to focus on what the doctors told her to do. She took unsteady breaths as tears of fear and pain wracked her entire body. In and out, she breathed into the bag. Her chest ached as if a huge man was lying on top of her. She clenched her eyes and willed the thoughts away. It was mind over matter. She had to remember that.

Her stomach muscles were tight, her body so constricted she felt like she could break into a thousand pieces. She kept forcing away the memories of the attack, her fears that brought on this nightly trauma and kept breathing and trying to think happy thoughts. The morning sun was already beginning to push against the shades and light, thin lines of sun penetrated through the tiny holes in the shitty old blinds. She chose this small apartment in the back of a small gift shop because it was hidden and no one even knew it was there but the owner, Helen.

She was a nice lady who didn't ask questions, and who knew her uncle, Tom and aunt, Sue. Essie hadn't known that Helen knew her aunt and uncle when she'd caught sight of the small "For Rent" sign in the storefront window when she'd first arrived in town. She hadn't wanted to stay with her aunt and uncle, just in case Blade somehow found her. She shivered, but at least her breathing was calming to a more natural pace.

She lowered the bag from her mouth and sat there on the floor, her feet tucked underneath her and her hands on the floor in front of her, just breathing and pushing away the aches and pains these panic attacks brought on.

When she tried to get up, she felt how weak she was. She didn't bother to force the strength that wasn't there to come. These episodes debilitated her. She probably would have wound up in a mental institution if the man had raped her instead of beating her. Thank God he hadn't, and to this day, she still wondered why. What was it he'd wanted from her? She'd never dated him, never even spoken to him beyond the few times after the night they met. She just didn't like him or feel an attraction to him, but Blade kept coming around. He kept trying to talk to her, or watch her. Then after the attack, when the police had gone through her apartment and found that he had been there, they'd also found the cameras.

He had been watching her. While she slept. While she dressed. While she showered. She felt so violated. It was as if he'd taken everything from her, including her whole life in New York, and she'd never even dated the man, kissed him, or really knew him. It was sick, and the only thing he hadn't seemed to rip from her was her virginity. He would take that, too if he ever found her. She was alone in this world now. She couldn't trust a soul or get too close to anyone, or they would be placed in danger, too when Blade finally found her.

She shivered. She pulled the hooded sweatshirt tighter. She no longer dressed in light clothing for bed. No matter how hot, or how sure she was that he wasn't watching, she couldn't let her guard down even as she slept. A prison. She was living life in a prison. But when she walked out that door and went to work, went to the dojo, or spoke with Helen, Precious, or the people she'd recently met, she pretended to be normal. Acted like a professional young woman working hard, taking care of herself, and new to this lovely town in South Carolina. They knew nothing of the turmoil she went through every day and every night. The fake smile, fake show of confidence. It was harder to show that confidence in the dojo, and definitely around certain men she'd recently met.

She swallowed hard and focused on her breathing and clearing her head.

She didn't want to think about Blade's capabilities. Of what she'd learned from the detective who couldn't prove shit. That Blade was a soldier relieved of his duties on a dishonorable discharge for assaulting his commander and threatening to kill him. She didn't want to think about his frame of mind, of how Blade was resourceful and so slick that even the detective feared his capabilities. It became clear after the attack that she wasn't safe in New York, or anywhere nearby. She had no choice but to leave her perfect job. To disappear in the middle of a night, wearing a disguise, acting like some secret agent, instead of being able to live a normal, successful business life as a twenty-four-year-old woman.

She worried constantly about naked pictures or videos of her showing up on the internet that the man had been taking. It made her shiver with disgust. How could he do that? How did he even get into her apartment and set those cameras up? The detectives explained about his capabilities as Special Forces, yet they still seemed unable to prove that it was Blade, and still questioned her part in this situation. How many times had they asked her if she'd had sex with, dated, kissed, or led the man on? Assholes. She never led him on. She'd been honest from the start and declined his offer of a date.

The man destroyed her success, her life, her everything, because of some fucked up reason Blade chose her to become his obsession. He took her independence, her ability to achieve and to fight, away from her. He turned her into this—a sniveling, scared, timid, panic on a moment's notice woman.

She slammed her hand down on the rug.

Eight months and she still had these freaking attacks. She'd thought she was getting stronger. Felt the training at Magnum's dojo was making her mentally and physically stronger, but then every night she had these. Every morning she woke up like this. She was so sick of it. She wanted to move on with her life but was afraid of her own shadow. She was afraid to make other friends, and when she forced herself to go out—like the night everyone celebrated that Precious had been safe and survived being abducted—she was scared.

She couldn't even converse with anyone other than Magnum, Carlyle, Cavanaugh, and Precious. She even shied away from conversation with Ronin and Bobby. Forget about those huge friends of Magnum's, the Stames brothers. Holy shit, when Turbo came over to talk to her and some of the people from the dojo, she slid away and made an excuse to leave, then snuck out and headed home.

She shook her head. Those men were gorgeous, hard, incredible, mysterious men. It didn't help either that the class she knew she should take, the self-defense one, was now being run by Ford, Max, and even Cobra. They were all Special Forces soldiers, and all she kept thinking was, Blade is Special Forces, too. Some one-man army and killer. She felt her throat tighten up, and realized that just thinking about the Stames brothers made her feel panicked and sick. Just because they were soldiers, didn't make them potential psychopathic killers. Look at the Mather brothers, and Magnum, and even at Bobby and Ronin. All soldiers, all normal. She swallowed hard and reached into the drawer for the energy bar. She shifted on the rug, feeling the energy slowly come back into her body and eliminate the weakness. She opened the bar and took a bite. She leaned back, and in between bites, took sips from the large water bottle she kept on the bedside table.

She looked at the clock. She wouldn't make that seven a.m. class. It was six a.m. It would take thirty minutes, maybe, to fully recover from this. Then she had to get dressed, eat, walk, run or bike to the dojo. She closed her eyes. Excuses. All excuses based on her fears. She wanted to take the self-defense class, but she didn't want to take it with one of the Stames brothers.

She felt her heart race. They intimidated her, put a fear in her so badly, and she didn't know why. Well, she kind of did know why. She found them attractive. She couldn't help but seek them out, and check them out. *Jesus, I'm such an idiot. One psycho soldier stalker, and*

I'm attracted to four total badass soldiers that no one, not even Precious knew much about. What Essie did know, was that they were resourceful and somehow finagled the capabilities to charter a plane, organize, initiate, and complete a mission and save Precious's life.

She couldn't even get through one night without a panic attack thinking about the man who had beat her to near death and still looked for her now. She didn't even trust the police. This town had a lot of police. A lot of soldiers, a lot of good people from what she had seen so far. She sighed and ran her hand along the dark blue rug. None of it mattered. She was timid except in the boxing class. She put on a strong, confident face in public, amongst Precious, who was badass herself, and in front of her boss, who was sweet as could be, even allowing her to take the back office, and never really have to show her face or socialize with customers.

That was sad, and she hated that. Essie had always been a people person. Tears filled her eyes. She played with the rug.

She was different. She was fearful, discouraged, and she couldn't break this cycle.

She leaned her head back and cried. *I'm not making the seven a.m. self-defense class. I just can't risk it.*

Chapter One

He stared out the window of the cabin, while he sharpened the blade of his hunting knife. His mind traveled a thousand places. The visions like photographs snapping quickly through his mind. Images of death, fire, pain, and the feeling of helplessness, then going ballistic. He blinked as the shots, so loud, so real, echoed in his head. He jerked, feeling the power of the gun in his hands, his arms, the numbness in his fingers as he unloaded his weapon into the sea of enemy soldiers.

He turned right, left, then center, clenched his eyes tightly, and then blinked until he saw her image. He tightened up. Froze at the sight of those gorgeous dark blue eyes, her luscious lips, delicate nose, and petite size. An angel. His angel.

His heart pounded hard and fast. He felt so desperate to see her in person. That's all he really wanted to do. His mind snapped back to that evening. His desire to touch her, to be close to her, talk to her was too much to resist. He knew he shouldn't. They had talked several times, and she shyly kept her distance as if she knew the evil within him and wanted to stay clear.

He shook his head. Rocked back and forth on the chair and dropped the knife. He gripped the arms and the flashbacks of the night he nearly beat her to death pulled him in. "No. No. My angel. I nearly killed my angel."

He saw her bloody face, her beaten body—the angel now a monster, and he did that to her. He lost control and the images in his head identified her as an enemy. He'd reacted. He left her there to die, but she didn't die. He tried to make it up to her. He broke into her car and left her things. He had watched her for so long before he made that stupid move and went to see her that night. He fucked up. He screwed up a simple recon mission to evaluate the situation, gain intel on his target, and prepare to make a move. But the flashbacks hit him instantly. The quiet city streets, the darkness, and his ability to camouflage with the night sent his instinctual training into a time warp of sorts. He lost his head. He was back in the desert, and his mind created a scenario that wasn't real. Essie became a target, instead of his quest for help and peace of mind. He nearly killed his angel. When he finally snapped out of it, he heard her whimpers and sobs for help, and when he reached down and turned her onto her back, he lost his breath at the sight. A bloody mess. He left her for dead and ran from the scene.

It took days for him to come out of his hole, and he would stare at her bedroom, at every room in the apartment waiting to see her. He knew she'd survived. He knew what hospital she was in and that hardly anyone but her boss came to see her. She was alone, and she needed him, but he was the one that put her there.

He waited. Didn't eat, didn't drink, and was nearly delirious with hunger when she finally arrived back home. He watched her painstakingly go through her daily routines, and he saw her battered, bruised body and cried. The black and blue marks over her breasts, her belly, and her ribs. God, he broke her ribs, he had to have, they were so discolored, and she held them with each step she took. Her naked flesh was no longer pure and beautiful, but battered and ugly, done so by his hands, his rage, his inability to keep his fucking head screwed on tight.

He would make it up to her. He had to.

Then weeks passed, and he tried bumping into her to say hello, and the look of fear in her eyes told him that she knew. She knew he had been the one to hurt her so badly.

He tried sending her gifts. He even put things in her car. She called the police. The fucking police were assholes. Then the detectives got involved, and they found the cameras he'd planted in her apartment. All of them.

He raged for hours. Pissed that he couldn't watch his angel. Couldn't see the body he would claim as his own. That he would care for and scatter kisses over, and own. She would be his saving grace. The one to clear his mind of the demons that made him want to do things. To hurt people, to act out on his rage.

But without the cameras, he couldn't watch her, and he lost his shit. He broke into her apartment, heard her answering machine go off with messages from two men who wanted to take her out to dinner or hang out with her. She was his. He stabbed the pillow numerous times, leaving the knife, and leaving her a message that they weren't through and she belonged to him. To him and no one else. He wanted to hunt down those men and kill them but didn't know their names. He never did find out who they were. It didn't matter. She disappeared, in the middle of the night, to a place he had yet to find.

"Where are you, angel? I need you so badly. I want to make it up to you. To protect you from all others set to do you harm." He licked his lips. Thought about her on the dance floor with her friends. They were slutty. She was sweet, sexy, but conservative. She had one hell of a body. Large breasts, slim hips, all of about five feet four inches tall, and those eyes. Those eyes set his heart, body, and soul on fire. She hadn't even known he'd set those cameras up in her apartment. Hadn't known he'd watched her. His mistake was not being able to hear her. To listen as she slept, her arm above her head, her thighs exposed, and even her pussy as she slept only in a T-shirt.

His cock hardened. He fucked up. He lost his fucking mind, a thing he just couldn't control no matter how hard he pushed the visions away.

He slammed the table. He felt desperate. Oh so very desperate.

"I'll find you, angel, and when I do, nothing else will matter but having you. Heart, body, and soul, forever."

* * * *

Ford Stames was driving down Beach Road thinking about his cousin, Slayer. He was supposed to be here a month ago, and still no word. They were a team. Ford, his brothers Cobra, Max, and Turbo, along with their cousin Slayer. Slayer was resistant to change. Ford understood that, and he knew a lot of Slayer's fears of settling down and trying to transition into civilian life were because of his experiences and the loss of his brother, Weiller. They all lost a good man that day in the war zone. Their cousin, just like Slayer, was more like a brother.

Slayer had a lot of issues. He didn't like to socialize and wouldn't be forced to. He liked to train. Felt that every day needed to consist of some form of training, even mentally. Cobra and Turbo shared that idea, but Ford and Max seemed to be pulling back from those soldier-mentality ways, and transitioning to being prepared, but fitting in. Taking on the self-defense training at the dojo was a huge step in doing just that. Though, because of their sizes and their strict, demanding attitudes, many of the people signing up for the program either loved it or hated it.

As he came to the red light before the small business district, he caught sight of a woman—blonde hair, business skirt in black, high heels, white blouse, carrying a briefcase and a black leather satchel. He had to do a double take. *Essie.*

He saw her walk to the front door of a small building. As the traffic light changed, he watched her disappear into the place and read the sign. It was some sort of insurance agency. Maybe that was where she worked?

As he continued down the block, he pulled into a parking spot by the café. He thought about her. She was beyond shy when it came to him and his brothers, but the woman was gorgeous. Young. Super fucking young, compared to them, but they all noticed her. They talked about her after the celebratory party at Carlyle's the night they all celebrated Precious being okay and surviving the abduction. Essie stayed clear of them. He actually thought maybe she liked Bobby and Ronin, but that wasn't the case. They said they asked her out and she declined. Something about not dating, but Ronin mentioned the way she kept a distance and seemed to not like social settings. He and his brothers, Cobra, Max, and Turbo all tried starting up a conversation with her, but she stuttered, looked around for an escape route, and finally just disappeared.

He knew they were big men, and a lot of women flirted with them that had the guts, but they kept to themselves, too. Essie was special. There was something in her gorgeous dark blue eyes that called to him. His instincts told him she was scared, and maybe just wasn't experienced with men. They were older. He didn't know what it was, and he shouldn't let it bother him that she seemed scared of him, but it did bother him.

He got out of the truck and headed into the café for a coffee. While he waited, he wondered why she didn't try to take the self-defense class. He noticed other women who took the classes Essie did at the dojo gave it a try, but not Essie. Was it because he and his brothers were the instructors? He felt the scowl from on his face, and as the door chimed indicating someone was coming in, he locked gazes with Essie, who stopped short, looking petrified. He realized he was glaring at her. He quickly gave a smile, but she had already turned away.

"Good morning, Essie. The regular?" the woman behind the counter asked.

"Yes, please, and Mo would like two jelly donuts, and Terry a toasted bagel with cream cheese," she told the woman, and he wondered who the people were she ordered for.

"No problem. I'll grab your coffee so you can have it as you wait," she said.

"Thank you, Denise," Essie stated, and then she waited and wouldn't look at him.

He didn't like that. She was avoiding him, and he wondered why.

"I missed you this morning," he said to her, and she swung her head toward him looking shocked. Denise, the woman behind the counter, said her name and smiled, watching him flirt with Essie. Denise gave her a wink.

"Excuse me," Essie said to him softly. She was sweet, absolutely sexy as damn hell, and he towered over her. He imagined snagging her around her waist, hoisting her up against his chest and off her feet, kissing her breathless. What in God's name would she do if he did that? She was the kind of woman a man would keep right by his side, would lift up into his arms and carry across a puddle, hell, a woman who needed protection. She was so darn sweet and feminine.

"I missed you at the self-defense training class. Thought you would be there," he said to her, and she worried her bottom lip. He hid his smirk and took a sip from his to-go cup of coffee.

Essie looked at Denise, who smiled wide and then went about preparing the order for Essie.

"There's a class tomorrow," he told her. Ford couldn't help but gaze over her body. When he looked into her eyes, he could see they were a little red, and he stepped closer.

"You feeling okay? You look a little tired." He leaned a hand on the counter next to her hip. She worried her bottom lip and then picked up her coffee cup, side stepped from him and took another sip. Then she hardly held his gaze when she responded.

"I never said I was interested in going to that class."

"Why not? It's a great class every woman should take."

"Then why do so many men take the class?" she countered.

"It's a great workout, and the men who do take the class also help instruct. We've been pretty crowded and want to make sure every woman gets the techniques correct," he told her and swept his eyes over her top. She was modest, conservative, but well-endowed. She couldn't hide it so much in the gym attire.

She took another sip of coffee, but it seemed she did so out of nervousness.

He squinted at her.

"You know I have many years of training, as do my brothers Max, Cobra, and Turbo. We know what we're doing, and we like to train people to be able to defend themselves or at least have a fighting chance. A beautiful, sweet, young woman like you should be prepared. Don't have the attitude that nothing bad could ever happen to you."

Her eyes widened and then she exhaled. It didn't feel right. Her response, that look in her eyes of surprise, or maybe it was that he hit the nail on the head and she had experienced something where she had needed to defend herself. His mind went from one crazy worry to the next.

"Why do you take that kickboxing class?" he asked her before Denise said the order was ready.

Essie thanked her and then took the bag, Denise smiling at the two of them, and Ford gave Denise a wink.

"Have a nice day."

"You, too, and good luck," she said, and it seemed to surprise Essie.

Essie looked at Denise.

"Honey, if you aren't interested in taking a self-defense course with this guy, then I'll do it, and I have a bad knee," Denise said, and Ford chuckled. Essie started heading toward the door. Ford hurried to open it, his arm above her shoulder, and he looked down into her eyes as she turned back toward him.

"I'm not interested."

"Your friend was."

"So go back in and see if she wants to be another one of your trainees."

"Hmm, jealous?" he asked. She stopped short on the sidewalk and looked up at him.

"I'm not jealous."

"Really, because you look a little flushed," he said and reached out to caress her cheek. Her lips parted, and his heart hammered inside of his chest.

"Damn, you need to take my class with me."

"No." She turned around and continued walking. He followed.

"Why not?"

"It doesn't interest me."

"Which part?"

"I don't know, the rolling around on the mat with some strange man who just wants to roll around on a mat with different women and feel like a macho, big guy," she said.

"What?" he asked and chuckled. She stopped again, turned, and looked up at him. She was shaking.

"I don't want to go to the class. I don't want to have a conversation with you. I just want to be alone, and go to work."

He placed his hands on his hips.

"Scared, huh?" he pushed. Her eyes widened, and then her lips tightened.

"What?"

"You're scared. I get it. Afraid that you could get hurt? Afraid that it may be too difficult for you to handle?" he challenged.

"I'm not afraid of the class or of you."

"Well, then I'll see you tomorrow morning at seven. Don't be late, or you'll have to do extra laps and push-ups. Have a nice day at work," he told her and glanced at the sign above her office door, giving her a wink and heading back down the sidewalk. When he turned to look back, she was staring at him, then headed inside of the front door to the office. Now he knew where she worked and where she went for coffee before work. He would make sure he bumped into her again.

* * * *

Once Essie got to the office in the back room, she closed the door and fell into her chair. She covered her face with her hands.

What have I done? That crazy jerk got under my skin and made me react. He got me angry, and I actually spoke back and didn't fold under. How the hell did he do that?

Shit. What am I going to do? Precious can't take that class yet. She's still recovering from her injuries, plus Magnum wouldn't let her until she was five hundred percent better. She smirked. Precious was so lucky to have Magnum, Cavanaugh, and Carlyle. She was envious, but the thought of even dating scared the bejesus out of her. She shook her head and then thought about Ford. She wasn't going to show up at that class tomorrow morning. She would go to her regular Saturday morning class. His challenges didn't matter to her at all.

Chapter Two

"He's here, and he doesn't even tell us anything or let us know?" Turbo asked Cobra. Ford and Max sat by the island getting ready for dinner.

"He texted that he was in the area but had to stop by and take care of something. That he would be here tonight," Cobra replied and then prepared the burgers to go on the grill.

"He texted. That fucking can't be good," Max stated and then took a slug of beer from the bottle he drank from.

"Let's not assume the worst," Ford stated diplomatically. Cobra exhaled and felt that uneasy feeling he always got when Slayer was around. He wanted his cousin permanently with them, not running off on dangerous missions with a fucking death wish. He was trying to keep his opinions and feelings to himself, but it was high time he sat Slayer down and told him enough was enough.

"Anyone else feeling antsy?" Max asked. They all looked at one another. The mood changed dramatically the second Cobra informed his brothers, his team, that Slayer was in town.

"Um, guess who I bumped into today?" Ford said and then rubbed his hand along his beard smirking.

Cobra stared at him, and then Turbo and Max shook their heads.

"She even say hello to you, or did she avoid you like she avoids the rest of us?" Turbo asked with an attitude.

Ford smirked.

"Well, I didn't give her much of a choice this time. I kind of cornered her by the café on Beach road. Turns out she works right down the block at this insurance agency."

"What happened?" Max asked, and Cobra tried to ignore the upbeat feeling he instantly got every time Essie was mentioned. He listened as Ford told his story about meeting her in the café, teasing her, and then challenging her.

"What made you do that?" Max asked.

"I don't know," he replied and played with his bottle of beer.

"I do. You don't know how to handle rejection," Turbo stated firmly.

Max laughed.

Ford gave Turbo a sideways glance. "Really? Like you handle rejection well?"

"I don't get rejected," Turbo stated with cockiness.

"Um, bro, Essie turned you down, too. If I recall correctly, she practically ran from Carlyle's bar that night," Max teased. They chuckled, and Turbo tossed a chip at him.

They were quiet a few moments.

"Do you think she'll show up?" Max asked and then cleared his throat. He was acting like he didn't want anyone to think he was a wuss for hoping what they were all hoping.

"I doubt it. We scare her," Turbo said.

"I don't know. I kind of got this feeling this time, like I got under her skin and she reacted," Ford replied.

"Great, so you turned her off by being aggressive," Max said to him.

"Actually, I was flirty and smiling the whole time. I got this feeling, though, like she's scared in general. I don't know. Maybe I'm just reaching, hoping, you know?" Ford admitted then took a slug of beer and looked away, seeming embarrassed for sharing his feelings.

"Well, I guess you'll find out if your tactics worked," Turbo told him, and then they got all quiet again. Cobra couldn't help but feel a bit worried. He, for one, was fine with being single, or so he thought until he'd laid eyes on Essie. Those dark blue eyes of hers told so much. That body, her long blond hair, sweet smile, and feminine attributes just seemed to pull him in.

He had his share of women over the years. Thinking about that made him feel like it was him that wasn't good enough for the likes of her. He tried to clear his head. This damn woman wasn't showing any signs of even liking them, never mind being attracted to them. Figures they would finally find a woman they all wanted, and she didn't want them. He turned toward his brothers, all looking somber.

"So, who is going to make the salad and the spinach while I get ready to cook these burgers?" he said, and they all got up ready to help with dinner as usual. Cobra glanced at the clock and wondered when Slayer would arrive.

* * * *

"Helen, this garden is looking incredible. I don't know how you do it," Essie said and bent over to look at the large tomatoes beginning to turn red.

"It's the soil. I've been using this soil for years, and it gets better and better each season," Helen replied and started pulling out some weeds. Essie inhaled.

"It smells so good. Fresh lettuce and tomatoes for salad, zucchini and squash, too. I would cook up a storm. Do you jar things also?" she asked.

"I do a lot of jarring and will definitely be doing so. You be sure to take whatever you want, Essie. I have more than enough for me, and I usually wind up giving so much away."

"Are you sure?"

"Definitely. You'll see in another week or so how abundant this garden will be. We'll be throwing things out from them rotting. We won't be able to pick fast enough."

"Oh no, I would cook them up and freeze them," she told Helen and Helen smiled. "Have at it, honey," she said and then her eyes widened, and her lips parted as she looked past Essie and behind her. Essie turned, shocked to see a man standing there, and a very large, handsome-looking one at that.

"Slayer. Oh God," she said and wiped her hands on her apron and went right to the man. Helen was in her fifties, but the man looked to be in his thirties. He was big, wore camouflage pants, a black T-shirt, and had tattoos along his one arm. He was definitely military. Helen and he embraced and Essie watched.

Helen stepped back and held on to his arms.

"Thank God that you're okay."

"I told you I would be," he said to her, his voice deep, hard, and somehow effective. Essie felt it bubble over her skin and to her core. He looked at her, and Helen chuckled.

"How rude of me." She pulled the guy, Slayer, by his hand toward Essie. She instinctively stepped back, and he squinted at her. Helen smiled.

"It's okay, Essie, this is Slayer. He was very good friends with my son, Kyle."

"Kyle?" Essie asked.

"Yes, he died in combat a few years back. He and Slayer were in basic training together and Special Forces training, too."

Slayer looked her over. She was still wearing her work clothes. He reached his hand out for her to shake. She shook his hand and gulped. He stared at her. "Nice to meet you, Essie." He said her name and, Jesus, it affected her like when Ford, Cobra, Max, and Turbo said her name. Why the hell did she think of them right now? She smiled and pulled her hand back.

He just stared at her, and Helen smiled wide.

"Essie is renting the apartment behind the gift shop."

"Really?" he said softly and gazed at her from head to toe again. Essie felt her cheeks warm and looked at Helen.

"I'll let you two visit," Essie said and then reached for her bag and purse she had put down on the bench.

"Why don't you join us inside?" Helen asked her.

She turned around and saw that Slayer—*oh God, what a name*—looked very serious.

"That's okay. I need to get changed and figure out dinner."

"Come on inside. Don't be silly. Slayer just looks like he bites. He's actually a complete gentleman and a soldier to boot. No safer place to be with him nearby," Helen said and started walking down the path toward her small house that was next door to the gift shop. Essie looked way up at Slayer. He had dark, blondish brown hair that was a little longer in the front. His eyes were dark brown, and he motioned with his muscular arm for her to walk ahead of him. She did, and couldn't help but to feel like the man was checking out her body. She should have declined the invitation, but Helen was so sweet. She looked over her shoulder at Slayer as she held the door open for him. His arm brushed over her shoulder, and she felt the attraction. What the hell was going on with her? She walked into the small, welcoming house and saw the pictures around the place.

"Come on in and sit down. Slayer, if you want a beer instead of sweet tea, I do have some in the ice box," she told him.

"I'm good with sweet tea, Helen. Thank you," he said but kept his eyes on Essie, then looked around the room and exhaled. It seemed to her that he felt comfortable here.

Helen started to make the sweet tea as Essie and Slayer stared at one another.

"Slayer just got back from a mission, or do they call it something different now that you're not officially active duty?" she asked him.

"Freelance work really, but still for the government," he told her, then turned to look at the pictures on the wall. Essie was staring at one of two men in uniform looking like teenage boys. She did a double take. Was that Slayer?

"Ahh, that's a great one, Essie. It's Slayer and Kyle when they graduated from boot camp," she told her, and Essie picked it up and looked at it. Kyle was gorgeous, too, and Slayer looked happy, optimistic, a bit different then this Slayer. He seemed harder. Probably military life. She felt tightness in her chest. She knew not all soldiers lost their minds and became stalking psychos, but it made her feel scared of them in general, and there wasn't much she could do about that.

"God, we were babies," he whispered from over her shoulder. He placed his hand on the picture frame, and she released it to him. She went to move but then felt his hand on her hip.

"You were babies. Fresh out of high school, ready to take on the enemies of the world," Helen said and brought over the sweet tea and began to pour it in the glasses.

He set down the picture, and Essie walked to the table. She felt the loss of Slayer's touch on her hip and it surprised her. Then he pulled a chair out for her to take as Helen smiled wide.

* * * *

Slayer couldn't believe the way he was feeling right now. He had difficulty coming here to see Helen, but she had been like a mom to him, and her son was his best friend. He couldn't believe the years that had passed since Kyle had died. He hadn't thought he would be able to go on when that happened, but he did. The fight within him, the promise to fight until there was no more fight left inside of him made him go on. Things were changing, and maybe the fight within was weakening. He had a lot to think about, and before he faced his cousins, he knew he needed to see Helen and let her know he was home.

It made him feel better if that were even possible. He hadn't expected to see her talking to a beautiful young woman, who sounded so sweet and sincere in her compliments about Helen's garden. He looked at Essie right now. Her dark blue eyes sparkled as she spoke to Helen about the garden again.

Helen smiled at him.

"I'm so happy that you stopped by to see me and let me know that you're okay. I worry so much," she said and then looked so sad. He reached out to touch her hand and was shocked, because so did Helen. Essie smiled at the two of them.

"I know you worry. I told you not to, but I guess you still do anyway," he said to Helen.

"Of course I do. I know you engage in dangerous activities, Slayer. I wish you would slow down, hell, quit."

He sighed, feeling that familiar heaviness in his heart. "There's so much to be done."

"There are others to do them."

"Helen," he said her name and hoped she didn't go on one of her rampages about him giving enough of his life and when was he going to focus on himself. He didn't know how to do that. He just knew how to be a soldier.

Essie leaned back and took a sip of her sweet tea. He watched her lick her lips and, holy shit, his dick hardened just like that. She stared at him and then looked away.

"So, how do you know Helen, Essie?" he asked her. He didn't know why. He wasn't the kind of guy to initiate conversation, and especially not with a woman. He never really had to. Women threw themselves at him, and he caught them if he needed company. That thought was all wrong here, with Essie. He knew that immediately. She was young. Too young, and, Jesus, virginal.

Helen looked at Essie and smiled. Essie did the same. "Well, let's see. Essie has been renting the apartment now for about four months. Right?" she asked Essie and the lovely blonde smiled softly.

"Yes. In fact, four months this Friday, and I will drop off the money for the rent at the store after work, if that's okay?"

"Don't worry, dear, I trust you," Helen said, but Slayer didn't. He thought maybe a little investigation was necessary, just to ensure Helen wasn't being taken advantage of in any way.

He leaned back and licked his lower lip.

"You work around here?" he asked her.

"In town."

"Doing what?" he asked.

She swallowed hard and looked panicked. His gut instincts kicked in as he narrowed his eyes at her.

"Where do you work?" he asked slowly and firmly. She just stared into his eyes.

"An insurance firm on Beach Road."

"What exactly do you do at the insurance firm?" he asked, wondering if she was going to try to trick Helen into some sort of insurance scam, or maybe get her to change things around with her personal items.

"I'm an underwriter, but it's temporary," she told him.

"You're good with numbers?" he asked her.

"Very good, but I enjoy marketing better. I like helping companies to expose their products to new clientele. It's what I used to do before."

"Where did you live before here?" he asked her, and she looked away from him and readjusted her shoulders, a telltale habit when she got uneasy or maybe lied.

"Way, way up north."

"Canada?" he asked.

"Not quite. So, what about you? Live and work around here?" she countered, obviously trying to avoid his questions. He stared at her and looked away. Now he was the one avoiding answering questions.

"Oh, I need to check the oven." Helen got up and walked further into the kitchen where the wall oven was. Slayer kept his eyes on Essie.

"Are you active duty?" she asked him.

"You can say that, doll," he said to her and she blushed. Holy fucking shit, she was sexy and sweet.

"Oh, damn it. The darn oven wasn't even on. Now the chicken isn't done. Shoot," Helen exclaimed.

Essie got up and walked over to the oven.

"It looks like it started to cook. Did the oven stop working?" Essie asked and put her hand inside to feel in there.

"It's not even hot. It must have turned off a while ago. Let me check the gauge, turn it on again, and see what happens." Essie closed it as Slayer got up and walked over. She was playing with the buttons when the oven came on immediately.

"Oh, there was a timer set."

"Yes, for one hour and forty-five minutes," Essie said to her and looked at Slayer.

"I think you may have put it in wrong, or something, because the oven is heating up perfectly now."

"Shoot. I can't believe I would do something so stupid."

"Helen, these things happen. It isn't a big deal," Slayer said to her joining them.

"It's past six o'clock. I was going to offer the both of you to stay and have supper with me. Now we won't eat until eight," she stated, sounding so upset.

Essie placed her hand on her forearm.

"That's so sweet of you, Helen."

"You would stay, both of you, if I asked, right?" she asked.

Slayer looked at Essie in her business attire—short skirt and white blouse—her tan legs on display. She was even wearing high heels, and he still towered over her. She was short.

"I would love to stay."

"I've offered before, I know you like your privacy, Essie, but Slayer is here, and he's like a son to me. It would be great for us to celebrate his return together," Helen said, and Slayer was shocked. He looked at his watch. The guys expected him. He should decline, but when he looked at Essie, she widened her eyes and clenched her teeth, lipping "stay," and nodded toward Helen. Was she threatening him, demanding he stay or else? He smirked and then raised one of his eyebrows up at her. She turned away.

"I'll stay. Let me just text someone real quick and let them know I have a change of plans."

"Oh good. Now about this chicken," Helen stated.

"Not a thing to worry about. We can fry it up, add some garlic, tomatoes, fresh basil from your garden, and turn it into chicken cacciatore. Do you have any pasta we can start cooking?" Essie stated, and Helen smiled.

"I'll grab some vegetables to go along with it, and you help yourself to whatever you need, Essie. Slayer will grab the pasta. He knows where it is," Helen said and walked outside.

Slayer was amazed at Essie's enthusiasm and how quickly she went to Helen's defense, even helping Helen as she did. It took away the bad thoughts and potential accusations he was forming in his head. He got the pasta, and Essie found a pot big enough for boiling water. She washed her hands, then filled the pot with water. She was facing the counter and looking out the side window of the kitchen to where the garden was, and Helen was picking things. He placed his hand on Essie's hip, felt her tighten and gasp. He pressed closer and whispered into her ear.

"You're very sweet, Essie. I hope this isn't some act to hurt Helen or trick her, because if I find out otherwise, I'll come after you personally."

She turned slightly, a look of shock and hurt on her face.

"Me, hurt Helen? Is something wrong with you?" she asked him, and he inhaled her shampoo, absorbed the sight of her gorgeous dark blue eyes, that narrow, feminine nose, and luscious lips. He wanted to kiss her, and it shocked the shit out of him.

"Oh God," she whispered, and he narrowed his eyes. She felt it, too.

"I grabbed a bunch of zucchini and squash, maybe you could—"

They looked at Helen, who stopped talking and then smiled so wide her eyes lit up.

She started to slowly walk backward toward the door. "I could go back outside if you need a few minutes."

Slayer felt too riled up to smirk, and when Essie moved away from him and began to chop garlic, he felt disappointed.

"We're good. I was just making sure that Essie knew how important you are to me. That way she keeps eyes on you when I'm not around."

"Oh, Slayer, you know I can take care of myself. Essie is the one who needs looking after. She's always alone and rarely goes anywhere. Maybe you could show her around town, take her to some of the famous places young people go," she suggested, surprising him.

"I can take care of myself, too, Helen. I choose to be alone. But, not tonight, so how about those veggies? Maybe Slayer can help?" Essie challenged.

He stepped closer to her and reached in front of her to the knife block, letting his arm graze her breast.

"I know a lot about knives," he said to her and she suddenly looked freaked out. He had been teasing, but apparently not that type of teasing.

"Let's get that pot boiling, and I'll help you cut those veggies."

* * * *

Two hours later and a few glasses of wine, they were laughing and talking up a storm. Essie couldn't believe how charismatic Slayer was. He had her laughing so hard she snorted, which sent Helen into a hysterical fit. She was practically drunk and Essie looked at Slayer when Helen began to doze off in the chair.

"I think we should call it a night," Essie said and stood up, causing Helen to awaken.

"Oh, oh my goodness," Helen said and covered her mouth. "I think I had too much wine," she added and giggled.

"It was a wonderful night, and I'm so glad you invited me to stay," Essie said and gave Helen a hug.

"You are an amazing cook, Essie. You're going to make a smart, wonderful man a very happy and lucky man, with that cooking," Helen told her, and when she pulled back, Helen pointed at Slayer. "She's a keeper. Be smart and don't let this pass you up." She turned around and gave him a hug.

"Come by when you can, Slayer. Good night. Oh, lock up behind you, oh…and walk Essie home, please. It's dark, and there's no light on the pathway."

She headed out of the room, and Essie grabbed her things. They turned off the lights, and when they got outside, she said goodbye.

"Have a good night, Slayer. It was nice meeting you." She started to turn, even though some deep, inner desire inside of her wished she could take a chance, but her anxiety and fears still ruled her life. Then she felt the hand on her arm.

"I was given a direct order to walk you home, ma'am. I intend to do just that," he said and guided her around the house and then across the way to the gift shop.

"Damn, it is dark back here. There should be a light out here. Anyone could pop out and grab you," he told her, sounding very upset.

"It's okay. I'm usually home before it's this dark, and besides, no one would be hanging around the gift shop late at night and down the side walkway."

"Sure they could be. Especially if they caught sight of you, a petite, pretty young thing walking alone. Someone could grab you, force you into your apartment, or try to take you."

She swallowed hard. She could feel how big his hand was, and as if he realized he was holding her firmly, he released her arm and placed his hand on her hip with his arm against her back gently. She exhaled.

"I'm okay, Slayer," she said, and as they got around the corner, something jumped out. She yelled and turned into his arms. He pulled her back, and they both heard the loud whine of a cat.

She gripped his shirt, and he held her snugly in his arms. She looked up at him. They locked gazes, and she was speechless, shaking, feeling like an idiot. Would he reprimand her some more? Would he say I told you so? What the hell would he say to her?

"You okay?" he whispered, then reached up and stroked her hair. She nodded. Like some mute, stunned by this sex god, she nodded. Duh.

She couldn't seem to say anything, and then he looked at her lips. She feared he might kiss her, and then hoped he would. She was curious as to what it would feel like, and right before his lips touched hers, she pushed him away and turned.

She walked backward and nearly tripped over her own bags she'd dropped at the sound and sight of the cat jumping across the way. Slayer grabbed her waist and pulled her close again.

"Whoa, slow down. I'm not going to hurt you," he told her and she shook her head.

"I...I think you should go. Now. Thanks for walking me." She stepped back, and he released her.

"I'll see you again, I hope."

"I don't think so."

"What if I want to see you again?"

"You can't. I'm sorry, Slayer, but I don't date. I definitely don't sleep around, and, well, I don't want any trouble. Good night," she said and grabbed her bags, unlocked her door, glanced at him one more time, seeing his shocked expression turn to one of confusion as she closed the door and shook her head. She leaned her head back against it after locking the door and the dead bolt she'd had installed.

"Why can't I stop being so afraid of every man, every soldier I meet? My God, he is fierce. Likable and fierce. An instant attraction, just like with Ford, Max, Turbo, and Cobra. Jesus, I'm losing my mind. My God, it has to be that I'm a virgin. There's no other explanation unless I have a death wish. Maybe that's what it is. Maybe I'm just not meant to be with anyone because no one can be trusted."

* * * *

"Where were you? We thought you'd make it home for dinner?" Turbo asked Slayer as he entered the house. It was after midnight.

"I got caught up in something," Slayer replied and dropped his large duffel bags onto the kitchen floor.

"Got caught up in something or someone?" Max asked.

"Does it matter? I'm back," Slayer told them.

He walked over to the refrigerator and grabbed a bottle of water. His cousins all gathered around the kitchen.

"You okay? No injuries?" Ford asked.

"I'm good," he said and didn't bother to tell them about the stitches from the knife wound to his side because it was just a slash—a close call. It was healed, and now an additional scar decorated his body. It was one of many.

He took a few sips of water and then exhaled. He looked around the large kitchen, then at his cousins. He focused on getting back to them, to here, and now that he was here, he didn't get that complete feeling he hoped he had. There was never a feeling of home, of belonging. He knew the reason why. Weiller was gone. His brother, his best friend, his twin.

"Well, we're glad that you're back. Your bed is all set and ready. Maybe later in the day we can sit down and go over a few things," Cobra said to him. He was the same age as Slayer. Thirty-six, and just about the same height, six feet three. He nodded and then leaned back in the chair and looked at his cousins.

"So, what have the rest of you been up to?" Slayer asked them.

"Nothing too crazy. Ford has been working on the stocks, and we made a few small investments locally. We can go over those with you this week," Turbo told him.

"We've been helping out Magnum at the dojo. Each of us helps instruct a few self-defense classes and some boxing instruction," Ford said.

He gave a nod. "Magnum is probably loving that. His place gets crowded, doesn't it?" he asked and took another sip of water.

"He expanded last year, has a second floor in the place, and runs classes from five a.m. to nine p.m. There are a lot of guys we all know going there now, keeping sharp, and some active duty needing new training. Magnum could use you for some of the more intense training that's up to date. He mentioned that you should stop in when you got back," Turbo told him.

He wasn't sure about that. He was a different person when he was battling, fighting, grappling, and working on the mats. His intensity could be lethal if he lost focus.

"Hey, why don't we let him get some rest, and over the next few days we can go over some stuff and have him check out the dojo. I'm sure Magnum and a bunch of the guys will be thrilled to see you," Cobra stated.

Max stood up first.

"It's good to see you, Slayer. I'm glad you're home," he said, and Slayer could tell his cousin was relieved, but he hadn't said much. Not like the others did. Max was just as affected by Weiller's death as each of them, and maybe a little more so because Max and Weiller served in the same command for years. He gave Max a nod and then one by one they started to head to bed, leaving Slayer, Cobra, and Ford.

"Breakfast is at six tomorrow. I have an eight o'clock class I'm teaching and tomorrow morning is my morning to make breakfast," Ford told him and then stood up.

"I'll jump right in on the schedule."

Cobra patted his shoulder and Slayer tensed. It didn't go unnoticed. It was a normal reaction of Slayer's to being touched by anyone. Cobra gave his shoulder a squeeze and a firm expression. "You're home now. It's a safe place, so remember that," he stated firmly, as a commander would. Cobra was smart, hell, all his cousins were, and they knew exactly what Slayer was all about. A loner, a man wanting to keep to himself and not engage in connections. They were the only ones he trusted and counted on, and was even having difficulty with that lately because of his emotions and the loss he felt.

They left the room, and he was all alone. Their home was a beautiful place. A nice retreat away from other neighbors and near the beach. With the open windows, he could hear the sounds of the ocean, yet couldn't see it through the windows with all the high grasses. It was a little bit of a trek down the path, then along a private path, but when the ocean and beach came into view, it was breathtaking.

He thought about tonight. About seeing Helen, Kyle's mom. He always got so nervous and felt a pit in his stomach and a sensation wondering why he lived and why Kyle, why Weiller and so many others, died. What was it about him that kept him alive? When would his day come? Did he even care anymore? This last job was intense, to say the least. The intel was shit, and he had to improvise, got caught in a shit of trouble, and lost his ride, then had to backtrack while remaining undetected, and it cost him a week's time. By the time he got to a safe zone to make a radio call, they couldn't send anyone back out for him for two weeks. Two fucking weeks he was stuck in the fucking desert, fending off thieves and enemy soldiers. All alone, and nothing to think about but death, and wonder when his time would come. When he got out, he headed to the base to be debriefed and got the knife wound checked out. He left the base and felt empty. Like he didn't care if he returned or not. It was the first time he'd felt the strong sensation that maybe it was time to retire.

He exhaled. He had even felt nervous, hell, guilty going to Helen's, to see her like he always did when returning from a mission.

She worried about him, and he appreciated that. Especially because he didn't talk to his own mom or dad. He talked to his aunt and uncles, though, and was certain he would see them in the next couple of weeks. They always invited the guys and him over for dinner whenever Slayer returned from a tour or mission.

He got up, turned off the lights, and grabbed his things. His mind still on the feelings he had coming home this time. From the way this mission went down, to the stab wound, the way he felt leaving the base and the command, to his visit with Helen and coming home, he knew things were changing. Hell, he was shocked to meet Essie and react the way he did.

He threw his stuff onto the floor, knowing tomorrow he would need to organize his shit and do a few loads of wash. He grabbed what he needed for a shower, liking that he had his own space, his own room, shower, and privacy. He thought of Essie again, and it bothered him. Sort of pissed him off. He just met the fucking woman, a small, feminine little thing with a kick ass body and a beautiful smile and—

He shook his head and turned on the shower, got undressed, and ran his hand along the nasty scar. It was super red and sore. He got into the shower and hung his head, letting the water beat off his body. He was tired, achy, and could use a week of sleep, but that wouldn't happen. He'd crash tonight from exhaustion, but then the nightmares would start, the fear would overpower his ability to just relax and rest, and he would fall back into the routine of being a soldier and sucking it all up. He thought of Essie once again. Of how it felt to meet her and feel an instant attraction. How when she licked her lips his cock hardened, and how hard she tried to ignore the attraction, yet still leaned into him. She felt good in his arms, against his side, his chest, and he felt triumphantly guilty when that big black cat jumped across the way a few feet in front of them, and she turned right into his embrace and grabbed on to him as if knowing he would protect her.

It fucked with his head, hell, with his body. Any other woman would have been offering him to come inside, and he would have been balls-deep in her cunt. He didn't get that scenario with her. In fact, he felt below her. Too old, too fucked up, too scarred for someone so young, sweet, and perfect. But goddamn was she special. He wondered what his cousins would think of her, and it shocked him.

"What the fuck?" he said aloud, grabbed the shampoo, and tried to push those thoughts from his head. That shit was years ago, hell, back when they were fucking crazy and on top of their world. They never took one woman together the whole lot of them, but they did take a few on two or three at a time, and it was pretty good. It was done out of that need to feel like they could let go and were still protected, had men to watch their backs as they sought the need for release. He never really let go. In fact, it had been a while since he'd had sex. When he did, it was meaningless. A way to ease an ache for him and for her. A fellow soldier, a nurse who didn't want any attachments but just a need for sex and to let go. It worked out, but it meant nothing.

Meanwhile, tonight, he'd just met Essie and had almost kissed her. She panicked. He smirked. She fucking panicked big time. He forgot how big he was, how aggressive and hard he was. The poor thing probably couldn't handle a man like him. He was fucking dreaming thinking she would even want a washed up old soldier like him. He shook the thoughts from his head and tried to finish showering so he could go to bed. Maybe thoughts of Essie would take away the bad thoughts that surfaced the moment his head hit the pillow? Maybe?

Chapter Three

"I know, Mom. I wish I could come by to see you and Dad, but I'm scared to take the chance," Essie said to her mother over the phone. Essie looked out at the boats in the marina. She used one of those burner phones and prayed it was enough to protect her parents and her.

"We miss you, and we worry so much, Essie. Uncle Tom and Aunt Sue say they haven't seen or heard from you either," her dad said.

"It's precaution, Dad. I can't take the chance of him finding me by screwing up. Plus, when he does locate me, I don't exactly want to put you and Mom, or Uncle Tom and Aunt Sue, in the line of danger."

"He isn't going to find you. The police and detectives are looking for him."

"You don't know that, Dad. They didn't do shit to help protect me."

"They've called several times looking for you."

"The police?" she asked and gripped the phone. Instantly, she felt the pain in her chest and an ache in her stomach.

"They say they have more information on Blade. That they've connected to his old commander in the military."

"Really? You mean the one he threatened to kill, went after, and wound up getting dishonorably discharged because of?" she asked, her voice raised.

"Honey, we're not the enemy. I know you're scared. If I was a better father—"

"No. Don't do that to me. Don't start with that crap, Dad. I know you love me, but you cannot protect me from a man like Blade. You know the deal. He's Special Forces. Let's not discuss it, and don't you dare tell those cops or the detectives where I am, or they'll lead Blade right to me."

"My God," he said, and then she heard her mom's voice.

"Baby, we miss you so much, and I pray this is over soon, and they find him."

Essie heard the alarm go off.

"I need to go. Time's up. Love you both," she said.

"Love you, too," her parents both said, and Essie disconnected the call. The sound of the alarm on her other cell phone continued to beep. She hated the sound. The sound embedded itself in her head as the tears fell, and she looked out toward the water. "I want to be free. I want my life back. Will that ever happen? Will I ever see my parents again, or will Blade win, and kill me?"

* * * *

"We got nothing. The other phone was untraceable. She's resourceful, that's for shit sure," Detective Brophy stated to Detective Rourke.

"The other fucking detectives failed her, that's why Essie and her parents won't trust us. Those idiots basically took this guy's side because he's military. Just a little digging and some questioning would have shown them that Blade, AKA Corey Flint, is a fucking time bomb waiting to explode. He's obsessed with this young woman. There's no other way to describe it," Detective Rourke replied.

"All we can do is keep trying to find this asshole and lock him up. He's going to screw up somewhere. If he's as desperate to find her and have her, he'll maybe do something else that will give his location away," Detective Brophy said.

"I hope that something else isn't murder, because right now, the path of destruction he left at his apartment alone is enough to put him behind bars and even in a psych ward for a long time," Rourke said

"How are those people? Did that guy, the landlord, get out of intensive care?" Brophy asked, feeling sick about what happened. How some sort of fight broke out and Blade went on a rampage and started tossing people left and right, stabbing them, including nearly killing the landlord before Blade escaped. He evaded police and the first detectives on the case with the assault on Essie Salter. They fucked up, and the commander put Brophy and Rourke in charge.

"He's on a long road to recovery. We need to start expanding our assistance in this case, Brophy," Rourke said, and Brophy understood what he meant. This was military related, despite Blade being discharged. Perhaps it was time to get further information on Blade and ways to track him down and catch him before Blade found Essie or her family.

* * * *

"Hey, beautiful," Ronin said to Essie as he welcomed her into the kickboxing class.

"Good morning, Ronin," she said and shyly waved at Bobby, Frank, and Gio who took the class. When she saw Precious walk in she was shocked. She smiled wide. "Precious? What are you doing here?" she asked, and the other guys greeted her as well. Precious smiled as Magnum walked in behind her and placed his hands on her shoulders. He looked serious. The instructor, Corey Jones, was behind him.

"She is slowly going to begin working out again," Magnum said, and he emphasized the word slowly. Essie smirked as Precious rolled her eyes. She stepped from his hands and opened her arms to give Essie a hug. The two embraced.

"I'm so happy to see you here. You take your time," she whispered to Precious. Precious pulled back and smiled. "I will, don't worry, and after class, we can hit the café if it works for you."

"Of course it does. It's Friday," she stated and was glad to have gotten through the week without seeing Ford and dealing with him saying he missed her in class.

"Awesome," Precious replied and turned to look at Magnum.

"Essie and I have plans after class, okay?"

"What about the sauna? You'll squeeze that in so you can relax those muscles."

"Yes, sir," she stated, and they chuckled.

"Okay, wiseass," he replied and then looked at Corey.

"You know the deal."

"I know the deal. She'll go easy, and if she pushes it, I'll yell at her."

"Nice, Corey," Precious said to him and Corey winked at her. Essie couldn't believe it. Corey was like a drill sergeant. He rarely smiled, wasn't exactly nice, and he demanded a hundred and fifty percent. Essie always left this class sweaty and exhausted.

"Let's begin," he stated, and they went to the positions and began the warm up.

* * * *

"So, she was a no-show all week. I'm telling you that you scared her," Max said to Ford. They stood outside of the kickboxing class watching Essie working out along with Precious, who Max was happy to see back in the dojo again. When class ended, they stood there waiting for Essie and Precious to come out. When they did, she stopped short and then looked away from them.

Precious locked gazes with them.

"Hey, how are you guys?" Precious asked, and Max stepped toward her and gave her a kiss on the cheek. "The question is how you are? I can't believe you're here. Are you sure you're supposed to be doing this yet?" he asked with concern.

"You sound like Magnum and his brothers. Believe me—I could have been here weeks ago."

"Happy to have a partner in there, Essie?" Ford asked her, holding her gaze.

"Like you, I'm happy she's feeling better and back to training," Essie replied, and then bent down to put her towel in her bag, and Max couldn't help but to eye over the deep cleavage of her breasts. Outside of the gym she wore modest clothing, and nothing too revealing, but in here she was dressed like most women who did intense training. Light amount of clothes because they sweated a lot and needed to stay cool.

"Well, we're headed out to the café. I guess we'll catch you here tomorrow," Precious said, and Max nodded his head but looked at Essie. Before he could say anything, Ford spoke to her.

"Hey, Precious, maybe you could convince Essie to take my self-defense training class. She hasn't shown up yet, and I think it would be a great work out for her," Ford stated and stared at Essie. Precious chuckled.

"I think if Essie wanted to go do it, she would. Right, Essie?" Precious asked.

"I like this class. I'm comfortable with this class."

"Maybe when I get the boyfriends' approvals that I'm good to go for every class, we can do that one together," Precious suggested to Essie. Max noticed Essie looked unsure, in fact, her eyes widened and then she looked down and away.

"Anyway, we're headed out. Have a good day, guys."

"You, too," Max said, and when Essie passed by, Ford gave her a smile, but she looked away.

"Jesus, she is super shy," Ford said.

"You're being aggressive. I think you intimidate her."

"Hell, Max, we intimidate everyone, but I'm going to keep talking to her and break her down. It may take months, but she'll come around."

Max chuckled.

"Maybe she's just not attracted to us like we are to her. Ever think that's the case?"

"No fucking way. I can tell she's attracted to us. I think she's really shy."

"Or there's more to it than that. She declines dates all the time."

"What the fuck? Someone asked her out?" Ford asked loudly. Max raised his eyebrows up at him, and Ford lowered his voice.

"When the fuck did you hear this?"

"I've been hearing it. A few different guys have been talking. She's really sweet, very quiet, but won't date."

"Maybe she's involved with someone else."

"Maybe. But I wouldn't keep pushing her. Let it be," Max said, and Ford nodded his head. His brother looked depressed.

* * * *

"Okay, I've been gone for two months. What gives? You still won't go out on a date with any of the Stames brothers?" Precious asked as they sat at an outside table at the café down the block.

"No. Of course not. Why would you even ask me that?"

"Essie, they like you, and you like them."

"I can't. You know why."

"I understand the fears, but that was back in New York. It's over," Precious said, and Essie looked away. She should probably tell Precious the truth so she would understand and help her to keep the Stames brothers from bothering her.

"Shit. It isn't over, is it?" Precious asked, figuring it out.

The tears burned Essie's eyes.

"Awe, honey, why didn't you tell me the whole story?"

"I was embarrassed. It's so crazy and stupid and unfair. I can't even live a normal life. I have to look over my shoulder, not let my defenses down."

"He's looking for you? This guy that was stalking you and attacked you?" Precious asked, raising her voice slightly and leaning over the table more.

"It's so bad, Precious, because the police never found him or could prove he was the one who attacked me and put me in the hospital, or that it was him who broke into my apartment and my car. Precious…" She swallowed hard before continuing. She trusted Precious and felt like she was a friend she could trust. Revealing everything out loud with Precious somehow made her feel nervous and worried that she could be making a huge mistake.

Precious touched her hand.

"What is it? Tell me. I won't tell a soul unless there's need to, like, this man shows up and you don't inform anyone, then I would have to tell to help protect you."

"I don't know if he will or not. He did so many things to ruin my life. To make me scared of all men, and especially military men. He broke into my apartment, left a knife in my pillow, a clear threat that he intends to do me further harm. Hell, kill me."

"The police and detectives couldn't charge him or get fingerprints off anything?"

"Oh, they did, and they also found…they found cameras."

"Cameras?" Precious asked and squinted. Essie couldn't even say the words as she pulled her light sweatshirt tighter and swallowed hard.

"Oh, Jesus, he was spying on you?"

Essie nodded her head. Precious covered her mouth and then shook her head.

"Jesus, this guy is sick."

"And a soldier. A wild, crazy, delusional soldier."

"You didn't date him or anything?"

"No! I spoke to him a few times at one of the bars and clubs my friends and I hung out at, but there was no attraction to him. Thank God," Essie said and ran her hand along her coffee cup. "If I had, I would be dead right now, there's no doubt in my mind."

Precious sighed. "Maybe we should talk to my men, to Magnum and Cobra."

"Oh God no." She shook her head "No, Precious, and definitely not them. Cobra and his brothers will think the worst of me. They'll assume I did something to bring this on, like most men, like the law enforcement officers back home assumed. They didn't want to believe a good-looking soldier would just pick a young woman like me to stalk. They kept giving me the third degree and I was the victim. They were insisting that I slept with him or led him on in some way and I didn't. It was frustrating and unfair."

"That sure as shit is unfair. What the hell?"

Essie wiped the tear from her eyes before it fell. She looked at Precious.

"I can't tell anyone. I just need to keep training and to be prepared in case somehow, someway he finds me."

"I don't like it. There's too much to worry about. You live alone, you work late sometimes, and you don't even have any training but the boxing."

"I would like to do more, but I'm scared. I used to be more confident, but the attack, being in the hospital for weeks and having this guy stalking me destroyed that confidence. I feel like I can't even follow my gut instincts."

"But you did follow those gut instincts and knew he wasn't right, and that you didn't want to get to know him."

"I didn't do anything wrong. I met him with friends, and we all talked, and I declined giving him my number or meeting up with him. Most guys take the not interested hint. This guy didn't. He took it to the extreme and the next thing I know, I have this guy showing up wherever I am. I wouldn't even accept a date with any guy I met out of fear he could turn out to be like this guy, or that worse could happen."

"So, you still feel that way now, even with men like the Stames brothers?"

"They're military like Blade is. They're big, like him, and capable like him, and there are four of them."

"Five I think. A cousin or something lives with them, but he's always on a mission. In fact, he came back recently, and they'll all be getting together at Carlyle's. I was going to ask you to come along. Maybe if you felt a little more comfortable with them, you could take that self-defense class. It would be an asset, and maybe help with that self-confidence issue."

"I couldn't do that. It's too intimidating, and I don't know how I'll react."

"Honey, women who have been raped have taken that class, and it's done wonders for their self-confidence."

Essie thought about that. She hadn't been raped. She was beaten and stalked, and it all scared her.

"I would take it with you, but that's going to take some time before my men let me. They're so protective."

"Of course they are. They almost lost you, and I don't blame them one bit."

"Come out with us tonight and see if you feel a bit more comfortable with them on a friend level. It's foolish to not take a class that can truly help you in so many ways just because the instructors intimidate you, or that you are attracted to them but fear getting involved with any man."

She looked at Precious and felt her heart racing.

"You have seen Ford in action, right? Flirting?" she asked. Precious chuckled.

"I have only seen him do that with you. In fact, I didn't even think those men date. You'll be safe with my men and me. I'll even have a talk with Magnum and be sure him, Cavanaugh, myself, or Carlyle are nearby at all times if that makes you feel safer."

"I don't mean to seem hysterical."

"Honey, you were victimized. It could have been worse, and this guy is still out there. Hysterical? Hell, you are brave and strong, and I'm amazed that you held this in and haven't told a soul. I think that maybe you're pushing the wrong people away when maybe you need to surround yourself with exactly what you fear the most. Capable, trustworthy, loyal soldiers."

Essie thought about that a moment, and as she looked away she spotted Slayer, and he spotted her. Her heart began to race at the sight of him. Black T-shirt, blue jeans, and wearing those cowboy boots sticking out from the bottom of his jeans. "Wow. Who is he?" Precious asked, and Essie turned back toward her, feeling her cheeks warm.

"A good friend of my landlord's. We just met the other night," Essie quickly told her as Slayer approached.

"Hi," he said to her.

"Hi," she replied. They held one another's gazes. Slayer didn't move to introduce himself to Precious and Precious chuckled.

"I'm Essie's friend Precious, and you are?" she asked, reaching her hand out.

Slayer shook her hand and quickly released it. "Slayer. Nice to meet you."

"Would you like to join us? I was getting ready to head out, but Essie is planning on lingering longer," Precious told him, and Essie gave her a look. She smirked and winked.

"Let me go grab a coffee and then I'll come back over. Nice meeting you, Precious," he said, gave a nod all straight-faced, and headed into the café.

"Why did you do that? Now he'll come talk to me."

"Because you looked like you do when I catch you staring at the Stames brothers. He is very good looking. Older, has that badass, don't fuck with me vibe thing going on strong. No wonder you're shaking," she said to her.

Essie looked at her hands and knew it wasn't the coffee.

"Exactly. He's a soldier. An active one."

"Yummy," Precious replied.

Essie harrumphed. "You're a negative influence."

"I think I'm a positive influence. We were just discussing you moving on and making friends. Just because you have coffee or a few drinks at a bar with a bunch of guys doesn't mean you're bound to them. It means you're making friends and getting comfortable. Make a new friend. Although, by the way he looked at you, I think you are already friends." She winked, and just then, Slayer came out with a coffee.

"Well, I am going to not be a third wheel."

"No, stay a few minutes at least. Just in case the conversation doesn't flow."

Precious exhaled as Slayer joined them and sat down right next to Essie. He looked her over.

"You go to a gym or something?"

"The dojo down the block." He nodded but something changed in his eyes.

"So, how did you two meet?" Precious asked, and Slayer explained. Then he and Essie talked about the chicken and Helen. They were focused on one another, and so Precious stood up.

"I need to go, but you two continue your conversation. I'll see you later, right?" Precious asked but gave her a firm look.

"Yes," she replied, and Precious smiled. "Nice meeting you, Slayer. See you around." Precious left, and Essie looked at Slayer, who didn't follow Precious with his eyes at all, which was a compliment. His focus was on her, and she started to feel a bit self-conscious sitting there in her workout clothes. The tank top showed more cleavage than she was used to showing off, and it was warm out. She didn't want to take off the light jacket.

"What type of classes do you take there?" he asked her.

"Kickboxing."

He raised one of his eyebrows up at her.

"What? You don't believe me?"

"Honey, the other night you jumped into my arms at the first sign of trouble, remember?" he teased her and her cheeks flushed. She lowered her eyes and he reached out and took her hand. She quickly looked up and locked gazes with him.

"Not that I minded one bit at all," he said, and she pulled her hand away from his and placed her hands on her lap.

"Are you always this shy?" he asked her. She looked up at him.

"I…I just like to keep to myself, that's all."

"I'm like that. I prefer to be alone most of the time," he whispered, holding her gaze.

"I'm used to it," she told him.

"No family?"

"I have an aunt and uncle who live not too far from here."

"Parents?"

"Back in New York, and you?"

"Helen, cousins, aunt and uncle, and I don't really talk to my parents."

"Why not?"

He stared at her.

"I'm sorry. I shouldn't ask that."

"Well, not unless you're willing to share more details about your life with me?" he challenged, and she felt nervous, but then saw his smirk.

She grinned. "So, what are you doing in town?"

"I needed to stop into the post office and then hit the hardware store before heading home. How about you?"

"Well, I'm running back home, cleaning up the apartment, making something small to eat because Precious and her boyfriends are insisting that I go out with them tonight."

"You don't sound too thrilled."

"I just don't like being at bars or clubs."

"I don't either. My friends are insisting I go out, too. Maybe we should ditch them all, and you and I can hang out?" he asked, and then looked surprised by his question. For such a hard, intimidating-looking man, he suddenly looked shell-shocked. "I didn't mean to say that. I was just speaking my mind. The alone thing, right?"

She smiled softly.

"It's better that way," she told him, and he squinted at her.

"You've been hurt by an old boyfriend or something?" he asked, shocking her. She swallowed hard.

"Shit. I can't believe I just asked that, too. Essie, I don't know what it is, but I'm sure as shit different around you. To be fucking honest, this is the most I have spoken to any woman, even ones I've slept with."

Her lips parted, and she leaned back in her chair. His words both made her feel excited and jealous. She needed to end this conversation.

"Well, I'm sorry, I guess."

He chuckled.

"It's me that's sorry. I'm going to get going. Maybe we'll bump into one another again?" he asked.

"Maybe," she said, and he stood up. She did, too, and pulled on her backpack. He eyed her over.

"You sure you don't need a ride back to your place?" he asked.

"I'm going to say no thank you."

He squinted at her. "That because of the comment about sleeping with women and doing less talking?" he asked, and she felt his eyes sweep over her body. Her breasts tingled, and her pussy actually throbbed.

She laughed. She couldn't help it.

"Bye, Slayer," she said, smirking.

He shook his head and walked away. She felt that giddy, silly feeling in her core. She thought about Ford and his brothers. They made her react in similar ways. Maybe Precious had a point. Maybe she could be friends first and then see where things led? Maybe.

An hour later, after Essie showered, dressed, and headed to work, she sat at her desk thinking about the café, and about seeing Max and Ford at the dojo. She went from feeling intimidated to curious, and then even guilty. She liked Slayer, but she also liked Max and Ford and found Cobra and Turbo attractive but scary. Now those two were big men and badass.

She heard the knock on her door and looked up to see Stewart, a coworker, standing there. He was six feet tall with wide shoulders, and not what she would expect from someone working at an insurance agency.

"Hi, Stewart, what's up?" she asked.

"Oh, just checking in and seeing what you're doing tonight. A bunch of people are going to Carlyle's," he said with his arms crossed in front of his chest, leaning against the doorframe. She thought he was a really nice guy and was always friendly. He didn't really flirt with her but did invite her out with friends knowing she was new to town.

She smiled.

"I'm actually heading there tonight too with friends of mine." He squinted at her.

"Who?" he asked, and she chuckled. He had taken on a sort of older brother role as he realized how quiet and shy she was. He warned her of what places to stay clear of and even avoiding specific bars even with friends.

"Precious and some guys from the dojo we work out at."

"Really? Not Ronin and Bobby, I hope," he said, sort of reprimanding her as if they weren't good enough for her and it was his business. She chuckled, blowing him off.

"They're just friends, and will probably be there." As she said that, she got a funny feeling and thought she better add something about not being interested in dating anyone at all.

"Besides, you know I don't date. It's just friends hanging out. I haven't been out in a while."

"Yeah. If I recall correctly, the last time you were out you were acting funny for the rest of the week."

She cringed remembering that. That was at Precious's celebration, and the Stames brothers had been hitting on her and trying to start a conversation, but she was a scaredy cat and wound up taking off.

"I think I'll be fine this time," she said and smiled.

"Well, I might see you there, so if you need anything, or any guys start bothering you, you get to me, and I'll scare them off," he said and uncrossed his arms and sort of flexed. She smiled but wanted to laugh. He was a big guy, but not as big or as capable as the Stames brothers or Slayer.

"I appreciate that, Stewart." He gave a confident nod.

"Well, maybe you'll let me buy you a drink this time. You'll like my friends. There're three women and four guys, all good people, and all live locally. They're involved with different businesses in the area, too. One of them is trying to promote this new line of water sports products. I was thinking you could give him some pointers because of your business experience you mentioned."

"Sure thing. I'll be happy to meet them."

He stared at her and looked like he wanted to say more. She felt a little funny and hoped he didn't like her and want to ask her out. The last thing she needed was an uncomfortable situation.

"Well, I should get back to work. I need to leave on time to be able to get ready for tonight. I have to hit the store on the way home, too."

"Oh, sure thing, doll. I'll see you tonight then," he said and then walked out of the room.

She went back to work and didn't give the conversation another thought. Her mind was on Slayer and the Stames brothers. Yikes.

Chapter Four

"Slayer, I'd like for you to meet our girlfriend, Precious." Magnum introduced Precious to the guy she and Essie met at the café the other day, and she wondered how Magnum knew him.

"Hey, Essie's friend, right?" she said and stuck her hand out to shake his. He nodded his head.

"Essie's friend? How do you know Essie?" Magnum asked.

"We met days ago at Helen's place. She rents the apartment from her in the back of the gift shop."

"Oh yeah, Kyle's mom. How is she doing?"

"Seems to be doing well."

"Great. I bet your cousins are happy to have you back home, too," Magnum said, and Carlyle came over, shook Slayer's hand, and then placed his hands on Precious's hips behind her.

"Wait, cousins?" she asked.

"Yes, Slayer is the one this gathering is for. He just returned from a mission and was gone for months." She smiled, putting it all together. Holy crap, Slayer was cousins with Cobra, Ford, Turbo, and Max and he lived with them. Jesus, Essie was going to have a stroke. Just then, she saw Essie arrive, walking in with Ronin and Bobby.

"So, how long are you going to be in town for this time?" Magnum asked Slayer, but Precious noticed that Slayer caught sight of Essie immediately. So did Ford, who went over to her and asked her something. She nodded, and he guided her toward the bar. But then Essie looked their way, saw Slayer, and Precious waved her over with a smile.

Essie touched Ford's arm and pointed over, and as they headed their way, Precious saw Ford place his hand on her shoulder. Precious wanted to pull her to the side and let her know that the guys were related, but it was too late. Ford made the introductions as his other brothers, Cobra, Max, and Turbo arrived.

"This is our cousin, Slayer. He's the guest of honor," Ford told her as Essie locked gazes with Slayer.

"Hey, sweetie. Long time no see," Slayer said to her.

"Cousins?" she asked him and then looked at Ford, who narrowed his eyes, and then Precious chuckled.

"Come on, guys, let's leave them alone," Precious said to Magnum and Carlyle.

"Leave them alone? No way, this is getting good. You know Slayer, Essie?" Carlyle asked despite Precious holding on to his arm and pulling.

"We met at the beginning of the week at Helen's place," she said to Carlyle and then pushed a strand of her blonde hair behind her ear.

"Monday?" Cobra asked. She nodded.

"So, she was why you were late arriving home your first night back in town?" Max asked and smirked.

"We just met, and things got crazy at Helen's. It was too much fun to leave early," he stated, still holding her gaze.

Precious smiled wide.

"Now, let's leave them alone," she whispered to Carlyle.

"Holy shit. I'll be damned. Good luck," Magnum said to Cobra and gave him a slap on his shoulders as he, Carlyle, and Precious walked away.

* * * *

Essie was shaking like a leaf. She couldn't look at any of them. Her mind was in a blur. It barely registered when Ford told Slayer that Essie was the woman they had their eyes on for a while now, but that she'd turned them down and was a no-show at the self-defense classes he trained. Then she felt a hand touch her hand and squeeze. She looked up, and Slayer was pulling her closer. He reached up and cupped her cheek.

"You like my cousins, too?" he asked her.

She looked at them surrounding her, then felt the hands on her hips from behind, and she tightened up.

"Be honest, honey. This is not some scam. This is fate," Turbo said holding her hips.

"You all seem like nice guys," she said, and Slayer shook his head. He stroked her cheek and glanced at his cousins, which was a complete shock to her still that they were related and probably lived together. Holy God. She teetered. Slayer pulled her against his chest and wrapped the arm that held her hand around her waist, keeping her hand locked with his hand and behind her.

"Easy, sweetie. This is a lot to take in, especially for me," he said. She tilted her head up at him, absorbing the scent of his cologne and the feel of muscles beneath her chest. She was glad she wore the skirt and nice top, plus the low heels. She had taken Precious's advice to heart and was going to try to be friends with the Stames brothers first. Now she didn't know what she was going to do. She was attracted to all five men.

"How about a drink and we sit down and talk things over?" Cobra suggested.

She had to be strong here. These were five military men. Big, sort of scary in a totally sexy, all muscles kind of way, but still capable, military men. She pulled back and took a deep breath. She looked at Slayer who was straight-faced and then Ford.

"I'm still not taking your self-defense class yet," she said to him and he chuckled. He placed his arm around her waist and smiled. He wore a beard well. It made him look rugged and sexy.

"We'll see about that," he added and winked, and she shook her head. Ford and Slayer led her to a table in the corner with high stools.

Ford assisted her, holding the stool as she got up and crossed her legs. They surrounded her, Slayer taking the seat right next to her and putting his hand on her knee. She looked at him.

"So, how does it feel to be back home and with your cousins?" she asked, trying for nonchalant conversation.

"Right about now, with you here, it's feeling pretty interesting," he said to her, looking at her lips.

"Slayer." She went to correct him, or reprimand him, or just try to get across to him, to them, that she wasn't accepting anything and was still declining any dates, but he shook his head, and she froze.

He ran his hand along her knee and leaned closer.

"No lies, no denials, just hang out and enjoy the night. Whatever happens, happens," he said to her, but she knew by the look in his eyes, and a glance toward his cousins that tonight wasn't going to be just any night. Things changed in a flash. Suddenly she wanted things she swore off out of fear.

* * * *

Cobra looked at Essie as she smiled then laughed at a joke Max told. Her eyes were so telling and the darkest, prettiest blue he had ever seen. Those thick, dark eyebrows and long, thick eyelashes made her eyes stand out even more so. The blue blouse she wore enhanced her eyes, and when her lips parted, it was hard not to stare and wonder what they tasted like. She had a sweet, soft tone of voice and a way about her. He felt like he needed to keep his hardness, his commanding tone in check. She was feminine and classy.

He didn't know what was really happening here. All he knew was that Essie affected all of them and especially Slayer. He never saw him so in tune to a woman, hell, another person. Slayer was still being quiet, but he kept caressing Essie's knee, and even Ford was stroking her shoulder. Then Max reached out and placed his hand on her thigh, giving it a tap as he told a story, then looked at Turbo, who shook his head with his arms crossed in front of his chest denying the events that were told. It was all so normal, and he wondered when it would go wrong? What would come of this attraction, and were they out of their minds? Essie was in her early twenties, and he and Slayer were closing in on forty.

"Would you like another glass of wine, Essie?" Max asked her.

"No, thank you. I have to drive home."

"We could give you a ride," Max told her.

She gave a soft smile and shook her head.

She started to slide off the barstool.

"I'm going to go use the ladies' room."

"Okay, we'll wait here," Ford told her, and they all watched her walk away. Cobra kept his eyes on her and the way some guys checked out her ass as she walked past them. He felt jealous, angry.

"Hey, what's with the daggers?" Turbo asked him. Cobra turned to look at him and his brothers. Slayer took a slug from his bottle of beer, leaning against the table, his arm still over the chair Essie had vacated.

"I'm fine," Cobra stated and then felt the hand on his shoulder.

"Hey, Cobra, you didn't even come over to say hello," Stephy said to him. She was a woman he'd met months ago. Her other friends came over, too, and were standing there trying to strike up a conversation with all of them.

As he turned to the right while Stephy carried on about shopping and then about trying one of the classes at the dojo and wondering which ones he taught or suggested, he spotted Essie. She locked gazes with him and then Stephy and the other women, and Essie had an expression of upset before she abruptly turned to the right, bumping into some big guy. He held her hips and turned her.

"Cobra, are you even listening to me?" Stephy asked.

"No. I'm not interested," he said and gave Slayer and Ford a nod to the right. They looked that way, but now he couldn't even see Essie, the guy was blocking her from them. Cobra started heading over there and caught sight of Essie. She was smiling and nodding her head, looking amused as the big guy talked to her a mile a minute. When he got closer with Slayer towering over the guy, Essie looked up at him. The man turned to see who was interrupting the conversation.

"Essie, is everything okay?" Cobra asked firmly.

"Yes, why?"

"We were standing there waiting for you and saw this guy blocking you in," he said and gave the man the once-over.

"Hey, buddy, I was talking to her. Want to go wait over there? I'm making progress," he said, and Essie rolled her eyes.

"Stewart, seriously?" she said to the big guy. He squinted at her.

"Essie, come on, go with it."

"No. This is silly. You probably know these guys or have seen them around. Cobra, Slayer, Ford, Max, and over there is Turbo. This is Stewart. He works with me at the insurance agency," Essie introduced them.

"Really," Cobra asked, arms crossed in front of his chest.

"It's temporary," Stewart said on the defensive.

"No, it isn't. You love it there," she scolded.

Cobra reached for her arm. "You coming back to the table?" he asked her, and she looked past him and at Stephy and the women who joined them without an invite, and then looked at them. She shook her head.

"Too crowded. You go on, though. I should mingle, catch up with Stewart, and then go see Precious and the guys before I head out. It was nice talking to you before," she said, then started walking toward the bar. Stewart gave them all a look and then headed with her.

"What the hell happened?" Cobra asked.

"I think we pissed her off," Max said.

"She got jealous because your flock of bimbos swarmed in as soon as Essie walked away," Ford said.

"I'm going to get another drink," Slayer told him and they parted ways, but Cobra kept his eyes on Essie. She sure did go from hot to cold fast. He remained nearby, and the moment Stewart walked away, Cobra came up behind her, wrapped his arm around her waist, and whispered into her ear.

"You're bored out of your mind with him," he told her and then ran his palm along her belly. She tightened up, feeling so feminine. He could wrap her in one arm and hold her snugly.

"I am not," she replied and turned sideways. His lips were inches from hers. "Honey, I am really good at reading body language, and I can tell you're bored. Lose the geek and come hang out with me for a bit?"

"I don't think so."

"There was no need to be jealous over those women. They ruined our good time."

"Who was jealous?" she asked him, slightly turning in his arms. He pressed her against the bar, and she stared up at him, her body sideways. He placed on hand on the bar caging her in on that side while he held her close with his other hand still firm against her hip.

"Isn't that why you didn't come back over?"

"No, Cobra, it isn't why. I told you guys I'm not interested in getting involved with anyone." He stared down into her eyes and at her lips.

"Why is that, I'm wondering," he said and stroked her hip.

"Don't do that."

"Do what?"

"Try to play games with me."

He stared at her perfect, youthful skin and he felt old, damaged.

"Your skin is beautiful. I can't stop touching you, or wanting you close," he said to her. She licked her lower lip.

"I want to kiss you." Her eyes widened.

"Don't."

"Why not?"

"Because it will make things worse."

"I think it might make things better," he said and leaned closer. She turned only slightly as if she was curious, too, and he pressed his lips to the corner of her mouth.

"Don't push me away. Push us away," he whispered as he pulled slightly back. She stared at him. She blinked her eyes several times. Her voice cracked.

"It's better this way," she said, and he didn't understand what she meant.

He shook his head and followed his gut.

"What are you so scared of?" he asked her. She just stared at him.

"You don't like me because I'm older?"

"What? No, why would you say that?"

"Is it because the five of us come as a package deal?" he asked, and her cheeks blushed. He stroked her hip and then up to her ribs.

"Honey, I'm the leader of that group. They're my family, my life, my everything, so don't play games with us. I don't mess around. The truth. Are you attracted to us?"

She sealed her lips and stared at him. She turned slightly so that she faced him and he kept one hand on the bar, his arm against her side and one on her lower back.

"Yes."

"Good, we're making progress."

"No, we aren't," she replied.

"Sure we are. All I need to do is find out what you fear about us and fix it."

She looked away.

"Is it our sizes? I know we're big men, but we can surely keep you safe and warm between us," he said to her and licked his lower lip as he stared at her gorgeous blue eyes. Her cheeks reddened.

"Cobra, this isn't a good time for me."

"Bad break up?" he asked, his gut clenching.

"I don't date, and I don't want to right now."

He reached up, stroked her cheek, and pushed her hair behind her ear. He saw the small diamond stud earring, and it was delicate and feminine like her.

"I need a better explanation than that."

"Cobra."

"Essie," he repeated, and she exhaled.

"Lots of things intimidate me about you and your brothers and Slayer. I'm going through some personal things right now and I'm not really a good judge of character at the moment, and I really think it's better if I just focus on me right now."

"Who was he and how did he hurt you?" Cobra asked her, and she looked shocked.

"Come on now. Does the dick live around here?" he asked and looked around them. "Point him out, and I'll kick his ass," he said, raising his voice.

She covered his mouth with her hand. "Stop that," she said, her other hand on his chest. He pulled her closer, and she released his mouth but kept her hands flat against his chest. He slid one hand over her ass and the other snugly around her waist.

"God, you smell edible," he said and sniffed her neck, making her laugh. She had a contagious laugh, and he couldn't help but to chuckle. Jesus, she was so perfect.

He kissed her cheek, her jaw, and then her lips. She turned away and gave his chest a slap.

"Cobra, I said I wasn't ready for anything."

"I think we're past that. Tell me about Mr. Asshole, so you can move on with Slayer, me, and my brothers."

She stared at him, his hold still firm. Her breasts pushed forward, and he could see the deep cleavage and a hint of her blue lace bra that matched the blouse.

"It isn't that easy. The only reason why I came here tonight was to maybe accept friendship, nothing more."

"You want to be just friends?"

"For now, for however long. I need slow."

"Honey, that will be torture unless you're talking friends with benefits," he teased, stroking her ass cheek as he nuzzled against her neck and suckled. She slapped his shoulder and pulled back laughing, her face bright red.

"Cobra, you are intolerable."

"You love it, though."

"No, I don't."

"Yes, you do."

"No, I don't."

"Liar."

"I'm not lying."

"I can tell you are."

"How?"

"You look to the right when you lie, or you're hiding the truth."

"Hmm, a military thing?"

"A man with experience thing," he said and pulled her against him closer, then kissed her again. This time she let his lips linger a moment before turning away. He was making progress. Thank God.

* * * *

"So, you decided to cut the Stames brothers and their cousin a little slack?" Precious asked Essie and Essie took a sip from her club soda. She held her gaze and then exhaled.

"I don't know what to do."

Precious touched her hand and gave it a squeeze. "If they're being too aggressive for you, tell them to give you space. Be honest with them. Maybe tell them about what happened to you and the danger you could still be in," Precious said to her.

"No. No way could I do that. That's a terrible idea."

"Why?"

"Why? Oh, let me see, hi guys, I like all five of you, I have no experience with men whatsoever, but the one guy I met at a club and only spoke to jumped me one night, beat the hell out of me where I wound up hospitalized for several weeks, and continued to stalk me. He invaded my privacy. Saw me naked, watched me shower, dress, undress, and even sleep, so I have issues with anxiety and freak out all the time when I'm alone. Oh, and I had to leave my home, my awesome job in New York, and hide out here in South Carolina, but that's not too much baggage, is it?" she said sarcastically and in a low tone.

"Okay, point taken, but maybe if you broke it down a little," she suggested.

"No. It's just better if I stay out of any kind of complicated relationship, hell, any relationship."

"Honey, it's too late for that. They have you on their radar. Heck, they're watching you right now."

Essie looked to the right to where she knew the Stames men and Slayer spoke with Precious's men. She locked gazes with Turbo and then turned away.

"I think I need to head home."

"It's Friday night, and you don't have work tomorrow."

"No, but tomorrow I wanted to do some cooking and jarring with Helen, and then Sunday I was thinking about going for a run, then hitting the beach to lay out. It's supposed to be the perfect day for that."

"The perfect day for what?" Turbo asked, joining them. He stood right next to Essie, and she tilted her head back to look up at him. His dark hair, matching scruff along his face, matched his dark eyes and thick eyelashes. He stared at her, and Precious spoke. "Just discussing weekend plans. So, you guys all live together near the beach, right?" Precious asked.

"On the back road and bend to Cliff Side Place," Turbo told her.

"Nice, I think Cavanaugh drove me up that way a while back. There's only one house up a side sand road. It's all private up there but looks like a hideaway. Really cool."

"That's our place," he told her, and Precious looked impressed as her eyes widened and then she smiled.

"Very nice. I bet there are great views from up there."

"Some of the best. Your boyfriends' house is awesome, too, though. Been there several times."

"It's very nice, and they keep it immaculate."

Cavanaugh called Precious's name, and she excused herself to walk over toward him. Essie took another sip of the seltzer and then watched some people dancing on the dance floor. They looked a little drunk. She felt Turbo step closer and place his arm around her waist. He leaned on the stool and pulled her between his legs, keeping his hands on her waist. In this position, she was almost eye level with him.

"What are your weekend plans?" Turbo asked her. She should lie. Make something up.

She couldn't. She wasn't a liar. "Helping Helen do some jarring with the vegetables from her garden, then Sunday a jog in the morning, and then I'm thinking about laying out on the beach for a few hours. Work on my tan," she said, looking at her arm. All these thoughts and emotions were bringing on an episode. She felt the signs. Why now? She really needed to head outside. He squeezed her hips and pulled her closer. She had to place her hands on his wide, hard shoulders as to not fall against him.

"I know a great spot, and it's private, too," he said, and she felt his hand ease along her ass then up her back. Did he mean their house on their private beach?

She looked down, and he moved a hand off her waist, she felt the loss, but then felt him clench her chin and tilt it toward him.

"It's really nice, and lunch is included, too," he said to her, stroking her jaw with his thumb. His hands were so big. The thought brought on mixed feelings—arousal, fear. He could do damage to her body.

"Hey, you okay?" he asked, obviously catching her expression of fear. She nodded. Turbo had such a seasoned look to him. He was tan, too, and there was something about his eyes that kept her engaged. She had to refocus on the conversation and keep her distance. She shouldn't let down her guard. God, she was so inexperienced it annoyed her. She was super sensitive and aware of everything when one of these men were this close and touching her. The size of his hands, his muscles, and how much smaller of a frame she had in comparison. Seriously, the man could snag her around the waist with one hand and keep her against his side like some trophy. She imagined Gaston from Beauty and the Beast, and how much larger he was to Belle, and how he could snag her up like nothing. The only difference was that Essie wasn't turned off by these men, but completely turned on and attracted to them. She was going to have a panic attack tonight. She just knew it.

"What is going through that head of yours right now, baby? You look petrified," he whispered, and he caressed along her lower back and ass.

"I think the public beach a few blocks from the apartment will do fine." She was surprised she remembered what they were discussing. He squinted at her and then gave a soft smile.

"I think you'd like our beach. Will you think about it?"

She shook her head. He seemed disappointed but surprisingly, he didn't push. She needed to put some space between them. Her heart was racing and her breathing funny. She knew the sensations well.

"I want to sit," she said as she pulled back, and he stood, pulled over a barstool, and watched her get up on it and cross her legs. She reached for her club soda with lemon and then looked around them. It was a nice gathering. Carlyle's was always so crowded. As she scanned the crowd, she spotted Slayer. He sat on a barstool in the corner just watching her. Their gazes locked and, Jesus, her nipples hardened and her pussy throbbed. She had to look away and recross her legs. She pushed a strand of hair behind her ear, and Turbo faced her.

"Do you work full time?" he asked her, and she nodded her head.

"How do you like the job?"

"It's okay. It pays the bills."

"Slayer mentioned that you did something else before when you lived up north. Where did you say you were from?" he asked. She realized that they talked about her, shared their conversations. Did it make her feel uneasy more than excited? She didn't think so.

"I didn't say. Just up north."

"Canada?" he pushed.

She took a deep breath and exhaled. Would it matter if she said New York?

He squinted at her.

"New York," she said and released a sigh. She couldn't believe how much better she felt revealing that to him. She came to this town, this state, out of fear and to hide from her stalker. It changed her in so many ways and had an effect on her personality, her responses, and reactions to people. The Stames brothers and Slayer caused stronger changes, reactions, and emotions in her. Could she tell them the truth as Precious suggested, or would they think she was a scaredy cat, an immature twenty-four-year-old pushover? Tears filled her eyes, and she couldn't hide it.

Turbo covered her hand that sat on her lap. She locked gazes with him as she stared up into his dark brown eyes.

"God, baby, I don't know why you're so scared, so shy, and unwilling to even have a simple conversation with any of us, but I can tell something is wrong. I want to know what it is. I want to know what you're so afraid of," he pushed.

Her eyes darted around them. They landed on Slayer, and he squinted at her and instantly slid off the barstool. She looked away and stood up. Turbo placed his hand on her hip. "Don't run away from me. Talk to me."

Slayer was there, and he looked so intense. God, the man always looked ready to kill. She shivered, felt her throat begin to constrict. She tried focusing on the music, the laughter. She ran her hand over her throat, closed her eyes, and focused on calming her breathing.

"Essie, are you okay?" Slayer asked, and his hand caressed her back, soothing the tightness. She nodded and just focused on breathing and on the feel of Slayer's hand caressing up and down her back and Turbo's hold on her hip.

"What's wrong?" Ford said, and she opened her eyes. Ford, Cobra, and Max all stood there.

"I need to leave," she got out and reached for her bag. She pulled from them and hurried through the crowd. She needed the fresh air, to get to her car and the paper bag she had in there. As she got to her car door, unlocked it, and stretched into the seat to grab the bag, she heard Slayer's voice.

"Essie, don't try to drive," he said to her, but she didn't respond. She scrunched up the bag and breathed into it. She inhaled, felt their presence surrounding her, and was so embarrassed. Tears hit her eyes, and her nose began to clog up. She begged herself to calm down when she felt the hand on her hip and the palm gently rubbing up and down her back. At first, she tightened up, but then she sensed the warm breath against her ear.

"Focus on taking small, easy breaths. You're safe here. I've got you. We all do, and no one can hurt you," Slayer said to her. She closed her eyes and did as he said. It was as if he knew she was having a panic attack and knew what to say, what to do. She kept her palm on the leather seat. She was bent over, and he was pressed against her enough to make her feel aroused and imagine being intimate with him, with all of them. She had to force those thoughts away, too and just breathe. When she finally felt like she was breathing normally, she removed the bag from her mouth and stood up straight. She ran her hand up her throat to her face as Slayer hugged her from behind. He kissed her neck.

"Better?" he asked, and she nodded.

"I'm sorry," she whispered.

"Don't," he replied.

She was afraid to turn around to look at him, at all of them. She was embarrassed. She blinked her eyes and turned to see them all standing there looking worried, and then they all smiled softly.

"You okay, sweetie?" Cobra asked. Tall, blonde hair, dark blue eyes and all muscles, the man looked like the Russian from the Rocky movies. She nodded.

"Want to go back inside?" Max asked. She shook her head and absorbed his good looks. He was all soldier from his nearly bald, short military cut, to his firm expression and perfect posture. He was tan too and filled with muscles, and she'd heard him talking to Magnum about a tattoo he had gotten a few years back. She wondered what it was and where.

Ford stepped closer. Despite the dark beard, brown eyes, and rugged woodsman look, he seemed the most compassionate and calm of the bunch of them. She felt comfortable with him.

"I want to go home, guys. I need to go. It's better if I leave now."

"I'll drive you," Slayer said.

She shook her head.

"Alone, Slayer. I can drive fine, really. It passed."

"You get these often?" he asked her as he reached up and stroked her cheek.

"Don't, Slayer. I'm embarrassed enough."

"Don't be embarrassed. Anxiety attacks are scary and just come on and are triggered by lots of different things," Ford said to her and she cringed. God, he was probably thinking crazy things right now.

"Are you seeing a doctor about them?" Cobra asked. Tears stung her eyes. She didn't tell anyone about them. Why would she, when even the detectives, the police back home couldn't find any evidence to prove that it had been Blade that attacked her that night, and that was stalking her, and who had broken into her car and her apartment? If she went to a doctor and they diagnosed her with anxiety attacks, the cops would think she was crazy and made things up about Blade. He was a man, a soldier, resourceful and looking for her still. She shivered.

"Essie?" Cobra said her name more firmly.

"I'm dealing with it, Cobra. It's none of your business," she snapped at him and felt bad. Then she looked at Slayer. "Thanks, and good night. Enjoy your welcome home party," she said and went to get into the car, but Slayer pulled her into his arms. He hugged her tight, and she tried not to hug him back, but he smelled so good and felt even better. She squeezed him and felt instantly emotional.

"You're not alone. I'm here for you, and I understand how it feels," he whispered to her. She kissed his neck and whispered, her voice cracking, "Thank you."

He didn't let her go. He kissed her cheek and then her lips. She held on to him, and he plunged his tongue into her mouth, and she gave in. She wanted to forget how stupid she must have looked and how embarrassed she felt, and instead feel Slayer's arms around her and him kissing her. He pulled her away from the car, ran his hand over her ass, and squeezed her to him. She couldn't believe how hard, how big his muscles felt against her body and her hands. She ran her fingers through the hair on the top of his head. The sides and back were cut super short, but it was longer on top. He ravished her mouth, cupped her breast and her ass at the same time, and she felt her pussy spasm. She moaned into his mouth, and she knew she needed to slow things down. He must have sensed her need to do that because he began to release her lips, and when they parted, she hugged him, pressed her cheek against his chest, and locked gazes with the others. Ford reached out, and she took his hand, brought it to her lips, and kissed his knuckles.

"I need time, guys. I'm not used to these feelings. I don't have any experience with men and definitely not ones like the five of you," she said, and Slayer eased back. She stood there still holding Ford's hand, and Slayer's hand was on her hip. He reached up and fixed her lipstick.

"We're willing to take our time. There's no rush, and when you're ready to talk, to let us in, we'll be here," Ford told her.

She was touched by his words.

"We're not going anywhere, Essie," Turbo said to her with his arms crossed in front of his thick, wide chest.

"Definitely not going anywhere," Max added.

"We'll work this out, Essie. All you need to do is let down the walls and let us in. It's that simple," Cobra told her.

She nodded and then looked at Slayer. She saw her lipstick by the corner of his lips. She reached up and wiped it away.

"Good night," she said, and he nodded. She got into the car, and he closed the door. They watched her pull out of the parking spot. One glance in the rearview mirror and she wished she had the courage, the faith in her gut instincts to let them in. To pour out her soul, explain about Blade and the terror she'd experienced, and to accept them into her life. But was it fair to them? Was it asking for trouble to be placed onto them, not if, but when Blade tracked her down? She was surprised by her thought pattern. When had she become protective of Slayer, Ford, Cobra, Max, and Turbo? She may not be able to resist getting involved with them after all.

* * * *

"What do you think?" Cobra asked his brothers and Slayer as they gathered around a table in the back corner of the bar.

"She definitely went through something traumatic. The panic attack was triggered by something," Ford stated.

"By us. We were too aggressive?" Turbo added.

"She reciprocated the kisses, Turbo, and she accepted each of us holding her in our arms, keeping hands on her all night. Something happened to her that is making her hold back and deny the attraction. It could be anything," Cobra said to them.

"I don't like the possibilities going through my head. She goes to the dojo and takes the kickboxing class, but she refuses to take the self-defense class," Ford told them.

"So, you're thinking she's trying to learn some defense skills but not engage in something more intense, like maybe just to build self-confidence?" Max asked Ford.

They were going round and round, talking things through, truly concerned over Essie. Cobra knew that they all wanted her and that this was different from anything they'd experienced before. They were older and had a lot of experience in life, with sex and trauma, and they could help her if they only knew what the cause of her anxiety was.

"What is the number one concern women have taking the self-defense training class you guys offer?" Slayer spoke up. He had been the quietest, and in the moment of confusion of what to do to help Essie during the anxiety attack, he got right in there and helped her through it. That in itself showed Cobra how special Essie was for touching Slayer and getting inside of his heart.

"Ford?" Cobra asked.

"I would say a number of things. Maybe the coming up from behind, and scenarios of a weapon being used, grappling on the ground, learning to get out from a position of being raped," he said, and his eyes widened. Ford sat forward.

"You don't think she was sexually assaulted, do you?" Max asked.

"Fuck," Turbo said and looked pissed.

"She's a tiny thing, so sweet and feminine. Hell, the average size man could do her harm, but men our sizes. Shit, we scared her," Ford stated.

"The only way to know is to ask her," Cobra said to them.

"She told me she was going to go for a run Sunday morning and then go to the beach. I tried offering for her to come to our beach and hang out, and joked about it including lunch, thinking we could spend some more time with her. She declined," Turbo told them.

"Of course she did. That's too intimate of a setting and secluded, too. A public place would make her feel more at ease if she has been a victim of an assault of any kind," Ford told them.

"What do we do? I like her. I want to get to know her and thinking about all this shit makes me feel protective of her. If we could get Essie to let her guard down just a bit, then maybe we all could show her that we'll protect Essie and care for her," Max said to them.

"We need to confirm something right now. Are we agreeing to pursue her as our woman? As a serious commitment, all of us?" Cobra asked and looked at each of them, and then at Slayer.

"I'm in a hundred percent," Ford said.

"Me, too," Turbo added.

"Definitely," Max said.

"I'm in," Cobra said, and they all looked at Slayer.

"Slayer, if you want to be part of this like I believe you do, it means making those changes you've been avoiding us talking about," Cobra said to him.

"You'd all be good for her," Slayer said.

"You would be good for her, too. You already are from what we all witnessed back there in the parking lot. Slayer. You met her separately from us at Helen's house and immediately were taken by her. This shit is special. Look at Magnum and his brothers with Precious. Hell, look at the James brothers and Rose," Cobra said to him.

"I've got my issues, though," Slayer said.

"Don't we all," Max told him and held his gaze.

Cobra leaned closer.

"You are a brother to us, not just a cousin. You're blood, have been a part of this family right here for years. We do everything together. We've shared women together, and you damn well know why it felt right and good." Slayer exhaled and turned away as if he didn't want to face that weakness.

"We all felt it, all needed that. To let down our guards so fully that we could let go and know our brothers had our backs. Why do you think ménage relationships are so rampant among soldiers and troops? It's because we're conditioned to be so fucking strong and have Teflon over our hearts that we have to constantly be on guard. But not in the bedroom when we make love to a woman and let it all out. We can let down those shields and just let go," Cobra said to them and they all mumbled in agreement except Slayer.

"We let go, and we fucked those women."

"At the time that was what we needed, Slayer," Turbo told him.

"What if I need to let go like that and I accidentally hurt Essie?" he confessed. Cobra swallowed hard.

"That's why we'll be there initially. This isn't a woman we just want to fuck. It's a woman who has touched us already and we haven't even felt her up," Cobra stated and winked.

"Speak for yourself. I copped a feel and, fuck, she is more than a handful up top," Turbo said to them and they chuckled.

"Hey, seriously, she's perfect. Probably too fucking perfect for the likes of us, but who the hell can argue with chemistry, and the intense attraction we obviously feel for her."

"Does anyone think maybe she doesn't have much experience with men, maybe not any, or what she does have was why she has panic attacks?" Max asked.

"Shit," Turbo said and then took a slug of beer.

"She is gorgeous, and has that virginal look about her that's more than just youthfulness," Ford added.

"A virgin?" Slayer whispered, and he looked fierce.

"Holy fuck," Turbo stated and released a sigh.

"Let's not make assumptions. Let's do what we do best and make a plan of action," Cobra said to them.

"What do you have in mind?" Ford asked.

"Shock and awe, brothers. Shock and awe," he said seriously, and they all nodded in agreement and began to discuss their plan of attack.

"We're soldiers, and we want Essie to be our woman. She's scared, hesitant, and we need to turn up the charm, let down our guard enough to let her know who each of us are," Cobra told them.

"Sounds like we have to act like a bunch of fucking pussies," Turbo stated. They chuckled.

"I'll do it. She's worth it. I never felt like this about any woman in my life, and I'm hoping she's the one," Max said.

"Then start tossing out ideas because if she's the one and she continues to be resistant, then we're going to need backup," Cobra stated, and they chuckled and then began to plan how they could win Essie's trust and her heart. They never failed a mission and they sure as shit weren't going to start failing now.

Chapter Five

"Stewart, I could get in trouble for this. Who is this woman and what do you want to find out?"

"Walt, she's the one. I'm telling you," Stewart told his cousin over the cell phone.

"If she's the one then why do I need to look up her personal information for you? Just do what normal men do and ask her questions when you're out on a date."

"I would do that, but she's resistant."

"Resistant?"

"Not like totally uninterested, more like scared. It's like she's been hurt before and I get this feeling that it was a man."

"No fucking way."

"Yeah. I want to find out so I can get through to her, make her see I can protect her."

"I don't know about this."

"Walt, didn't I come through on the low interest rate for the mortgage for the new house? That wasn't exactly a legit process."

"Shit. I knew you were going to eventually cash in on that favor. Okay. Give me her full name and what you know about her."

"Well, I had to look in the closed files. She's the only one in the office that has a closed file, but I think the boss knows her aunt or something. Anyway, her name is Essie Salter. She's twenty-four and lived in New York City. This was her address," he said and rambled it off.

"Okay. Give me some time to do this under the radar. I'll be in touch."

"Thanks, Walt. I appreciate it."

He disconnected the call and leaned back on the couch. He thought about Essie. She was sweet, young, professional, and she sure didn't need those five older soldiers ruining her reputation and her sweetness. Hell, they had to be pushing forty. Stewart was closer to her age, and he was just as big as those guys. He could probably take them if he needed to. He would wait to see what his cousin came back with, then he would make a plan to win over her heart.

* * * *

Helen smiled at Slayer. "So, you and your cousins really like her?" Helen asked. He nodded.

"I saw it in your eyes immediately, and in hers. She's so sweet and beautiful, but you should know, Slayer, I think she's been hurt before," Helen told him. They sat at her kitchen table talking as he found out where Essie went to lay out on the beach.

"I think so, too. She had an anxiety attack last night at Carlyle's," he told her and explained about what happened and how good things had been going. Helen scrunched her eyes together with concern.

"She added a deadbolt to the door on the apartment," she told him and he squinted at her. He cared for Helen a lot and had no problem talking with her. He wished he could talk to his parents that way, but it wasn't possible.

"Well, what's your plan with the guys?" she asked.

"We're trying to figure out how to each spend more time with her to ease her into a relationship. As she gets comfortable, we thought we would slowly add on. You know, two of us, three of us and then all of us. It's going to be torturous, but hopefully, the best way to show her we care and are willing to take our time."

"I bet you won't have to wait that long. She's a smart woman, and the attraction was instant between the two of you. Heck, I thought you were going to kiss her that first night you met her." She chuckled.

"I bet your cousins had the same reaction."

"They did." He played with the cup of coffee.

"What else is bothering you, Slayer?"

He looked at her.

"Just thinking about Kyle and even Weiller. How if they were alive they'd be part of this, too."

She covered her heart.

"Lucky little lady Essie would be. I would have set them up if he were still alive," she said and smiled.

"I'm sorry. I probably shouldn't have said that."

"Are you kidding? Like I haven't thought about the possibility the moment Essie showed up looking for an apartment? She's so sweet, gorgeous, and very appealing. I've seen the way men look at her." He narrowed his eyes at that.

"Sorry. You should know that no men ever came to the apartment. I've heard her decline offers of a date from some guy at work, too."

"Stewart?" he asked. She squinted her eyes.

"Actually, yes. How did you know?"

"He was at Carlyle's last night. Tried to act protective of her in case we were bothering her."

"Hmm, not competition, though."

"No," he said confidently, but it added to his concerns for her wellbeing. Maybe they needed to add bumping into her at work to the list of missions to win her heart.

"So, who is going to pop up on the beach to meet her?"

"Max," he said and smirked. She smiled.

"Sporting all his muscles and tattoos, I'm sure. Good choice. And today, when she and I are jarring vegetables and cooking up tomatoes?" she asked.

"That's what I was going to talk to you about."

She smiled.

"What do you need?"

"Just for you to have your cell phone with you. That way I can text that I was looking to stop by and see you with Turbo."

"Then what?"

"You ask her if it's okay for us to stop by. Then we do, and we watch you ladies do your thing and just talk with her."

"How about help us? That would be better and more convincing, plus working side by side with a woman in the kitchen can be considered foreplay."

She winked.

Slayer chuckled and felt his cheeks turn red. She laughed.

"I'm not that old or clueless."

"Never said you were, ma'am," he added.

"Well then. It's a plan, and I want to be posted on tomorrow's results, too."

"Will do, Helen. Will do."

* * * *

Essie was chopping up tomatoes and working on making the jars of sauces as Helen started chopping up the other vegetables, and even preparing to make jarred pickles, when Helen's cell phone rang.

Essie listened to the country music station Helen had on in the house and was enjoying the love song when she heard Helen say Slayer's name and then Turbo's.

She looked at her, her hands covered in tomatoes, and listened.

"Sure thing. I completely forgot about that. Come on over. We could use the help," Helen said then disconnected the call.

She was smiling and then wiped her hands and walked over to the cabinet to pull out more seasonings.

"Everything okay?" Essie asked and washed her hands, finished up the last set of jars, and then was going to get started on slicing up cucumbers for pickling.

"Oh, yes, just fine. Slayer and Turbo are coming over. They need to check my air condition unit in the bedroom. It was acting up and this upcoming week is supposed to be record heat."

"Seriously, it's supposed to be that hot?"

"Yes, and without proper air conditioning, it could really be brutal. How is your unit at the apartment?"

"It's not bad, but I do keep it at its highest level when I'm home. I don't leave it on during the day."

"Oh, Essie, you should keep it on so the place doesn't get too hot. Don't you worry about the electrical bill. That unit doesn't take up much," she said, and Essie thought about how it rattled and didn't really cool the place, but she didn't want to bother Helen over it. Perhaps she should have the guys look at her unit, too. She felt a bit uneasy. She was trying to keep some space and be friends first. She pretty much realized she liked them and was attracted to all five men. "It's acting up, isn't it?" Helen asked as if reading her mind.

"I'm sure it will be fine."

"I'll have them both look at it after they help us here."

Just then, there was a knock at the door, and Helen called for them to come inside.

They greeted them both, kissing Helen's cheek and then coming over to Essie and giving her kisses to her cheeks, and caressing her hips as they greeted her.

She didn't know they were coming over. If she had, then maybe she would have worn something other than the short shorts and the off-the-shoulder T-shirt with AC/DC on the front.

"It smells incredible in here," Turbo stated and then looked over the jars they already made and then winked at Essie.

She smiled softly and went back to cutting up the cucumbers for the pickle jars.

"So, the air conditioner is acting up in the bedroom."

"We'll look at it, Helen."

"Oh, and later maybe you can look over Essie's at her place? It's not a hundred percent, and with this heat wave coming I want to ensure she's comfortable there in the apartment," Helen said to them. Essie looked at Slayer, who held her gaze.

"We'll be happy to check it out," Slayer said, and he and Turbo disappeared into the bedroom.

She was quiet and couldn't help but feel excited seeing them again. They were both so attractive, and she would be lying if she said she didn't like seeing them.

* * * *

An hour later and after making several dozen jars of pickles, tomato sauce, and assorted vegetables, Turbo watched Essie take off the apron and then exhale.

"That's a lot of jarring," she stated.

Turbo placed his hand on her hip and pulled her back against his chest. She held on to his hands.

"It sure was, and we missed the first two hours, but it was fun," he whispered and kissed her bare shoulder. She looked casual, sexy, and smelled edible.

She didn't pull away. Then Helen spoke up.

"Oh, don't forget to check out Essie's unit at her apartment."

"Well, let's finish cleaning up here first," Slayer said.

"They don't really have to look at it. I think it will be fine," Essie stated.

"No, I insist. I don't want you to suffer if it breaks down. Slayer and Turbo know what they're doing," Helen said as Turbo released Essie and Helen winked at him

"If it isn't a problem and you have time," Essie said to him.

Turbo nodded.

"We don't have any other plans. It's a relaxing day today," Turbo told her. Turbo and Slayer carried two boxes of jarred food for Essie, and they said goodbye to Helen, then headed down the side street and along the path to the back apartment behind the gift shop.

Turbo couldn't help but to admire Essie's body in the short shorts and the washed-out blue T-shirt. He had wondered if she were even wearing a bra and then caught sight of the line of the back strap when she bent forward in Helen's kitchen. The woman was voluptuous up top.

As she unlocked the door to the apartment and went inside, Turbo felt the heat right away.

"Do you have the AC on now?" Slayer asked.

"No. I don't like to waste the electricity for it. It only takes about fifteen minutes for it to kick in and spread out to here," she told them, and then motioned for them to put the boxes on the counter.

"I'll take a look," Turbo said, and Slayer helped her unpack the jars and put some in the refrigerator and some in the closet.

Turbo went into her bedroom, her perfume filled his nostrils, and his eyes landed on her bed. It was a queen-size bed with a plain white bedspread and big, fluffy pillows decorating it. She didn't have any pictures on the walls, but her room was organized, neat, and clean.

He walked over to the air-conditioner unit in the wall and was looking for the power button but couldn't find it.

"Essie, where's the power button on this unit?" he called out to her. She headed into the bedroom with Slayer close behind.

"Oh, it's hidden in the back on the left."

He reached back there. "I'm not finding it."

Her bed was a foot from the wall, and she had to squeeze by him, climb onto the bed, and then lift up and reach back over the unit to turn it on. It started up.

She couldn't pass him, and he did that intentionally as Slayer sat on the edge of her bed.

"I don't feel anything yet," he said to them.

"It will kick on," she whispered and looked at them.

"This is a nice set up in here. You a clean freak?" Turbo asked.

"Me? No, I just don't have a lot of things to clutter it up," she said and then closed the slightly opened closet she stood by.

Turbo sat on the edge of the bed and lifted his palm toward the unit, not feeling much of anything cool yet.

"It takes time."

"It should pop right on," he stated, and she walked closer.

He took her hand and pulled her between his legs.

"Why don't you have a lot of stuff?" he asked her. She worried her bottom lip. He ran his palms up her hips then down her thighs. Back and forth, he caressed her.

"I don't know."

"Did you leave things in New York?" Slayer asked and leaned onto his side on the bed.

Turbo stroked her skin under her shirt and then her belly. He felt something and slightly lifted her up.

"What's this?"

She leaned back and ran her hand over his.

"Belly ring," she whispered.

"What?" Slayer asked and sat up to look.

"That is sexy," Turbo told her and ran his palm along the piercing and then lifted her up, lowered her to the bed, and then explored her belly with his mouth.

"Turbo," she said and grabbed on to his head.

"I can't resist. I had to watch this sexy body work in Helen's kitchen and all I could think about was kissing you." He then leaned up and kissed her mouth. She ran her fingers through his hair, and he felt the bed dip, and then Slayer joined them. His cousin ran his hand under her top, over her belly, and right to her breast.

She pulled from Turbo's lips and turned to the left only for Slayer to cup her cheek. "Hey, beautiful," he whispered and then leaned down and pecked at her lips as if testing her state of mind before he deepened the kisses.

They were moaning and exploring her skin, her breast when she pulled from Slayer's lips.

"Oh God, where did slow go?" she asked. Slayer and he chuckled as Turbo stroked her belly ring and then the crystal charm on it. It was feminine and sexy.

"Out the window the second we laid eyes on you. We can't help it, baby. The attraction is so strong. Can't you let us in and accept us?" Turbo asked and stroked her hip.

"I want to. I really do, but I need time for a reason."

"Some guy hurt you? Is that right?" Turbo asked.

She didn't reply.

"Essie," Slayer said her name and she looked at him.

"It's complicated."

"What in life isn't?" Turbo pushed.

"This is different," she replied and sat up. They did, too.

"How so? I mean, is he still a problem?" Turbo asked.

"Yes, but it isn't what you think."

"Then fucking explain, because if this guy has the potential to hurt you again or isn't leaving you alone, then we have a right to know," Slayer said all possessive like. It surprised Turbo. He was always more aggressive than Slayer. She pursed her lips.

"Slayer, this is why I'm not ready to explain it all."

"I want to protect you and be with you. Saying that aloud is not in my personality. Do you understand what I'm saying?" Slayer asked her.

She looked from him to Turbo and then took their hands and held them on her lap. She closed her eyes and exhaled.

"Part of both of your personalities honestly scare me, and also affect me."

"We don't want to scare you," Turbo said to her and used his other hand to stroke her hair.

"I know you don't, and that's why I need some more time. It's me, not you," she said and then brought their hands to her lips, and she kissed their knuckles. It was sweet just like Essie.

Turbo narrowed his eyes at her and looked at her body.

"This is torture," he stated very seriously.

She smiled and then reached up and cupped his cheek.

"For me, too if it makes a difference," she admitted and he nodded his head.

"I think the AC works," she said and started to get up.

Turbo placed his hand over her hips and belly, then lowered her back down to the bed.

"We should see how it works when the heat is turned up." He covered her mouth and kissed her, feeling so hard and hot. No amount of AC would cool him down or calm him down, but claiming Essie.

* * * *

Essie set up her umbrella for when it got too hot in the sun on the beach. She laid out her big blanket as well as the small cooler. She was glad she invested in the beach cart to carry all the stuff from the parking lot to the beach. As she started to put on her sunblock in the shade of the umbrella, her eyes landed on a guy with no shirt on and tattoos along his shoulder. He was tan, muscular and—

Her breath caught in her throat. It was Max. Holy shit, and he even had tattoos on his chest and one surrounding his belly. She looked away as he turned, preparing to sit on a chair and sunbathe. *God, what were the chances that he chose the same beach as her and the same spot to lie in?* she wondered, and then couldn't help but to think the guys were relentless in their pursuit of getting her to feel comfortable with them. She even discussed things with Precious this morning and explained about the anxiety attack. Precious gave great advice and Essie realized with her lack of sleep and full-fledged panic attack she had pretty much every morning, that she needed to make some changes.

She admitted to herself that she liked making out with Turbo and Slayer on her bed, and his idea of testing her AC to handle heat had been one hell of a test.

Then this morning while she was on her run, she bumped into Cobra and Ford. They jogged with her and talked about a bunch of things before they had coffee at the café down the block. Then they both kissed her breathless before leaving her to head home.

She knew they were strategically planning these little sessions of bumping into her. It didn't upset her. It made her smile and think how genuine they were and how they were trying to give her time. She liked all of them, and now that Max was here, she anticipated spending time with him, too.

She turned around and prepared her chair. She was glad she wore the royal blue bikini and even had her belly ring in. That, Turbo and Slayer definitely liked. She blushed from the thoughts of them playing with it and kissing her all over her skin. She heard a whistle and turned to see three guys walking by, close to her age, and checking her out. She ignored them until one guy walked so close to her blanket he kicked sand onto it.

"Hey," she said to him.

"Hey yourself, cutie. You all alone out here?" he asked, eyeing her over. His friends did, too.

"Take a hike," she said to them, and one of the guys whistled.

"A woman as sexy and beautiful as you should not be alone on the beach," he added. She felt a little concerned, but then someone came up behind him and slammed their hand on his shoulder.

"She isn't alone, asshole," Max stated, and the kid jumped.

He looked at Max as his friends hurried away, seemingly aware that Max was bigger, taller, and looked like he could kill them.

"Shit, sorry, man. Your girlfriend is hot," he told him and then took off practically running.

Essie placed her hands on her hips as Max gazed over her body.

"Fucking kid is right, woman. You sure as shit don't belong on a beach wearing that, and all by yourself with no protection."

"Who said I didn't have any protection, and why does it matter what I'm wearing?" she asked. He stepped closer, closed the space between them, and pulled her into his arms. She grabbed on to his forearms.

He gazed over her breasts, then her lips.

"Jesus, Essie, do you have any idea how fucking hot you are?" he asked her. She felt her cheeks burn. Her lips parted. He stared at her with a firm expression.

"Ask me to join you," he demanded.

"Wasn't that your point of coming here?" she countered, and he squinted at her.

"I was just going to lay out for a while."

"Same beach and same spot that I always lay out when I get the chance?" she asked suspiciously. He smirked and stroked her cheek.

"Baby, maybe we're not the only ones who think you should let down that guard and give us a shot." She took a deep breath and exhaled, but then felt his lips press against the corner of her mouth. He then whispered into her ear.

"Invite me to join you, please." He looked at her.

"Go get your stuff," she said. He winked, and her belly did a series of flips and flops. Jesus, he was lethal.

He released her, and she instantly felt the loss of his touch. As he went back to his spot to grab his things, she ran her hand over her belly, made sure she looked okay and then prepared to lay out in the sun. It was hard, though, as she took a seat on the blanket and he joined her, exposing all those muscles and tattoos, looking sexy, older, and protective as he stared at her body while she lay out in the sun. She could feel his eyes on her, and she prayed he thought she looked incredible. Thank you, Corey Jones, for being such a demanding kickboxing instructor.

* * * *

It took a bit of time for Max to get over his rage at those assholes who were hitting on Essie. Holy shit, what if he wasn't there to intervene? Would they have invaded her space entirely and forced themselves onto her blanket? Onto her? He was fuming still, but grateful he had been there and gotten rid of them. Her body was exceptional, and that belly ring, fucking sexy. He couldn't wait to tell the guys, so he snapped pictures of her as she lay, eyes closed in the sun looking perfect. He chuckled as he got the various responses from his brothers and from Slayer. They liked what he sent, but not that she was alone and random guys had hit on her.

"I thought you were here to lay out and relax," she said, her eyes still closed.

"I am relaxing."

"You're playing with your phone."

"My fingers like to keep busy," he said, and she turned to look at him, squinting.

"Are you all Special Forces?" she asked him, surprising him.

He turned onto his side to face her, and she did the same, causing her large, full breasts to push further from the skimpy top. He loved how she had definition in her arms and thighs, but it was her dark blue eyes and the expression on her face that drew him in.

"Yes, we're all Special Forces." He saw her swallow hard.

"That's an elite branch of the military, isn't it? I mean, you guys have capabilities that other soldiers don't have?"

He eased closer, reached out, and placed his hand on her hip. He stroked her hip, and she held his gaze. He ran his hand along her thigh, then up her arm and shoulder.

"Lots of branches of the military have special capabilities, but Special Forces are pretty badass," he said and winked. She smirked, and gazed over his muscles. He felt his cock harden. She reached out and stroked the tattoo on his chest.

"What does this mean?" she asked, and, holy Christ, the feel of her soft, feminine fingers on his skin aroused him.

"It means death before dishonor," he stated. She stared at his lips, and he inched closer. He stroked her hair from her cheek and then leaned closer, feeling her out.

"Max," she whispered.

"Essie," he said and smirked. She smirked, too, and then he pressed his lips to hers.

It was a soft, gentle kiss, and when he pulled back to see her reaction she seemed okay. "What else do you want to know about us?" he asked her.

She shifted on her belly, making him lose the great view of her luscious breasts, but now he could see her ass in that sexy blue bikini.

"You're all so serious all the time, especially Slayer, Cobra, and Turbo. Heck, even you. I think Ford is the most easygoing. Why are you guys so intense, and look like you're ready to kill someone all the time?" she asked. He raised his eyebrows up at her. She chuckled.

"Bad question?" He stroked her shoulder.

"No such thing as a bad question. I guess we are pretty serious. It has a lot to do with our training. We're taught to be on guard and expect the unexpected. Can't do that if we lose focus. Someone could get hurt or killed, or we could get hurt or killed."

"But you're civilians, not active duty, right? Is it post-traumatic stress, or something psychological?" She asked him, and his gut clenched. Was she involved with a soldier at one time who had PTSD and hurt her? He felt angry, sick to his stomach.

"I'm sorry. I shouldn't ask such things," she said and rolled to her back. "No, I want you to be honest and ask me, and the others, anything you want so you won't fear us."

She looked at him, and he leaned over, put an arm over her waist, and stared down into her eyes.

"Were you involved with a soldier that had PTSD?" Her eyes widened. She shook her head.

"You can tell me. I mean, if that's why you fear us, why you think we could snap and hurt you or something then I understand. PTSD is a serious disorder and if it goes untreated that person could become dangerous, aggressive, or obsessed." He saw the tears in her eyes, and then she rolled back to her side to face him. She whispered to him.

"Something happened, Max, but I'm scared to talk about it. I don't want to believe that you or your brothers and cousin could ever do me harm, but the fear is there for several reasons."

He caressed her hair and held her gaze. He wanted to know who hurt her and scared her so much.

"Baby, can you explain a little bit? This is the most you've revealed, and it's helping me to understand your hesitation in accepting us. Perhaps if you shared some details it would ease our minds and yours so we can move on and explore these feelings," he said. He stroked her shoulder and hip, then over her ass.

"I'm embarrassed," she whispered.

His heart ached. "You trusted this guy, this soldier, and he hurt you?" She shook her head.

"I don't understand. Help me to understand," he said. She swallowed and then began.

"I was out with friends. We frequented a few bars and clubs along this one strip in the city. We were familiar with the area, with mass transit, so we always went there and enjoyed dancing and meeting people. One night we met several guys, and this one guy, really big, and good looking approached me. I got this feeling. As he talked, it got stronger, and in all honesty, I didn't feel an attraction to him. I was polite, though," she said, and he figured she would be. Perhaps even a pushover if the guy was aggressive. She was just too sweet.

"Anyway, another night we were out again, and that same guy was there, and I saw him watching me. It put me on edge."

"Of course it did."

"I guess it was later within the week that I started getting these messages on my cell phone. Breathing, not words or anything, and then I'm out with friends, and he's there. He approaches and starts talking to me and asking me out. I tell him I'm not interested in dating anyone. He gave me the creeps and like I said, he was a big guy. He seemed upset, but he walked away. A few days later, someone breaks into my car. Some things were missing, like my lip gloss, a sweater I had in the back seat, not money or anything, so the police didn't think it was a robber. I mentioned the guy at the club, but they blew it off, said they would locate him, but I didn't have a full name, just knew him as Blade. That's what he called himself."

"Did you see him again?" he asked her.

Her eyes filled up with tears. She moved closer to whisper as if afraid someone might hear her. He was inches away and holding her gaze.

"I was walking home from work."

His heart was pounding. *Please don't say you were attacked and raped. Please don't say that. Poor, sweet Essie.*

"I was almost home when suddenly someone grabbed me. Put their gloved hand over my mouth and dragged me into the alleyway. I tried fighting him off, Max. I tried," she said as tears fell. He ran his arm over her waist and pulled her against his chest.

"He struck me repeatedly. Beat me until I was unconscious."

"What? It was the guy from the club?"

"I believe so. It's who I said I thought it was when the police and detectives questioned me a week later."

"A week later?"

"I was beaten so badly I was in the hospital for three weeks."

"Holy fuck." He ran his hand over her ass and lower back, and squeezed her to him.

"He didn't rape you, touch you?" She shook her head.

"I wondered why, and so did the police, but then after I recovered and was at work, and they said they couldn't find him, someone broke into my apartment. They tore the place apart and left a knife in my pillow. It was him, Max. I know it was him."

"Jesus, and the police couldn't find him?"

"No, and it got so bad because I was living in fear, having nightmares, the anxiety attacks that I have every night fearing that he will find me."

"Baby, you ran away from New York to come here to hide from him?" he asked as her red eyes watered more and she nodded.

"Fuck." He hugged her tight, and she sobbed against his shoulder. No wonder she was so scared.

"I had to leave there, Max. When the police and detectives were gathering fingerprints and looking for evidence," she said and then stopped. He stroked her hair.

"What?" he asked.

"They found cameras, Max. He was spying on me. Saw me naked. Saw me showering, sleeping, and…Oh God." She sobbed, and he held her close and rubbed her back.

"Son of a bitch. What a fucking asshole. The police couldn't find him?" he asked and she shook her head as he continued to console her. No wonder she was so scared of them, of letting down her guard.

"Honey, we would never hurt you, force ourselves on you, attack you, do you know that?" he asked her.

"I want to follow my gut and believe that's true and that I can trust each of you, but Blade was Special Forces, too, Max. He's big like the five of you, capable like the five of you, and the note he left stated that I was going to be his and he would protect me and kill anyone in his way of getting to me. I left my parents, my job, my life to escape. The police can't find him. He is looking for me, Max. I know he is, and all of this is why I can't let down my guard and get involved with any of you, or when he does find me, he'll kill all of you to get to me," she said, her voice cracking before she started to cry.

He held her against his chest and consoled her.

"I'm so sorry that you went through this. That this guy ruined your life." She wiped her eyes and pulled back.

"I never kissed him, went on a date with him, slept with him, and the police at first didn't believe me when I told them that. Then when he beat me and didn't rape me, they were all apologetic, but it was too late to try and find him. He evaded capture and will continue to do so. I'll never be free or safe as long as he's out there."

"But, baby, you can't live like this, fighting an attraction to all of us and being alone out of fear of this guy. We can protect you." She shook her head.

"It's my problem and not baggage any of you need."

"That's not your decision to make, it's ours," he stated firmly.

"Max, you're all older, more experienced, and why would you want someone who has a crazy stalker hunting her down?"

"Maybe because you need us, we care about you already, and won't let this dick get close enough to hurt you. Maybe this attraction is stronger than your fears, and maybe we're meant to be together."

"It isn't fair. I haven't dated anyone. I remain alone because it's better that way and I can't get control of these anxiety attacks."

"We can help you with those. Especially Slayer. He's had personal experience with something similar."

She widened her eyes at him. "Is that how he knew what to do to calm me?" He nodded and then stroked her jaw.

"I'm going to tell my brothers and Slayer about this, so they know and understand. Would you be willing to hang out with us? Get to know each of us so we can explore these feelings?" he asked her.

"Didn't you hear everything I told you? Why would you want a woman with all this baggage and fears? I might not be able to let you that close to me. I could freak out and ruin it all." She carried on.

He shook his head.

"Sweetie, this type of relationship is special, and all this shit that you've gone through isn't your fault. You didn't ask for it. This sick fuck chose you, and he's the one with the problem. You would be safest with us. With all of us."

"I'm scared, though."

"Rightfully so, but we want you, and I think you want us, too." He pressed his lips gently to hers and then she hugged him and he rolled to his back as she lay against his chest and exhaled.

"I'm so relieved that you didn't run away from me when I told you."

He chuckled. "What? Why would I have done that?"

"You're older, can get any woman you guys want. I'm twenty-four, and my experience with men includes a stalker I never even kissed or dated. That's insane to my own ears."

"You're twenty-four, gorgeous, and sexy, and to be honest, it's us sitting back wondering why someone like you, so perfect and beautiful, would feel an attraction to men like us. Older, washed up, and looking at forty," he said to her. She chuckled.

"I guess the attraction is just too darn strong," she said, and he smiled wide. He felt hopeful, and maybe, just maybe, Essie would be their woman in no time.

* * * *

Essie held Max's hand after they put all the stuff in her car and his things in his car. They walked down the side street, and she started to feel uneasy again. Her chest felt tight, her thoughts all scrambled. She should feel a bit relieved, having explained everything to Max, but she didn't. She still wanted to keep her distance to protect him, his brothers, and Slayer. Was it silly?

It felt right being with him, just like it felt being with the others. They were men. Older, sexually experienced men, and they would want to have sex with her. Want to possess her, make her their woman. This should be an exciting time, and yet her fears that Blade was looking for her still remained in the back of her mind.

Max stopped and brought her hand to his lips. He kissed her knuckles.

"Talk to me. What are you thinking right now?" He wrapped his arm around her waist and pulled her close. They stood by a bench as people walked by.

"That I shouldn't give into these sensations, to this attraction I have for all of you." He scrunched his eyebrows together and exhaled.

"Baby, you don't need to hide anymore. We'll protect you from this guy. We know a lot of people." He reached up and cupped her cheek.

"You do know that it was us that arranged everything to save Precious and rescue her?"

She didn't know the details. She just knew that they were resourceful. She wanted to believe him. She wanted to trust in him and his brothers and Slayer. She looked away.

"The police—"

"No, the police, those detectives, they have to do things differently than we do. We don't play by the same rules, Essie. We play by our own rules, and if someone messes with us, or someone we care about, we do what's needed. Now I'm only going to tell you this one time. I'm certain my brothers will, too, and Slayer as well. When we make a promise, we keep it. All we ask is for honesty, and for you to put that same trust in us that we put in you. Now, you're a beautiful, smart woman, and I know you're young, maybe haven't had many boyfriends or lovers, but with us, it will be different, and it will be perfect."

She couldn't believe that he thought she had boyfriends, lovers. Jesus, when she told them she was a virgin to boot, God only knew what their reaction would be. Probably hysteria. God, she wanted what he said to be true. She could see herself giving them all of her.

He stared down into her eyes.

"Tell me that you'll put these fears aside and give us the opportunity to prove to you that this is real and not some fling."

"What are the others going to say when they find out about Blade? About the danger I could be in, my fears, and then my anxiety attacks?" she asked, sort of rambling.

He gave a soft smile. "We're all different men, but we all want the same thing. To make you our woman, to protect you and keep you safe. They'll be pissed, and they may even act protective, just like my reaction, but they would never hurt you or force you to do something you weren't ready for. Understood?"

She smiled. "Understood." As they started to walk again she was still very nervous, but as she and Max talked about normal things, and even about their childhoods, she couldn't believe how compatible they were and how much better she felt. So when he walked her to her car and kissed her goodbye, she really believed she could give this shot, and that everything would fall together perfectly.

Chapter Six

"What?" Turbo raised his voice.

"You got this dick's name and information?" Cobra asked.

"Where is she now? Not alone, right?" Ford asked.

"Calm down and hear me out. It was a hell of a fucking day, okay. Not what I expected. To find out that Essie has a fucking stalker, and he's Special Forces," Max told them.

"Fuck. Who is he? Tell me you got a fucking name?" Turbo stated.

"Calm down, Turbo. She isn't in immediate danger. Let me explain how it happened, and what I know right now." Max explained, all the while his brothers listened, cursed, and paced the kitchen. Slayer remained straight-faced.

"She should be here with us now. He put her in the fucking hospital for three weeks. How the fuck badly did he beat her? She's a little thing," Ford asked then slammed his fist down on the table.

"You all need to calm down. We can't react like this around her. It will only push her away," Max told them.

"She needs protection," Turbo said.

"So, he wasn't a boyfriend, a guy she slept with, or fooled around with?" Cobra asked.

"No, and because the police thought she was lying or making shit up, it nearly cost Essie her life. Then he broke into her car, her apartment, and left a knife in the pillow. The cops and detectives never found this guy Blade," Max told them.

"I can call Callalow. He can get everything we need on the down low. Then, Slayer, you work your end with the connection." Cobra began to formulate a plan. Max knew they would initially want to kill the guy, but then would do their research and find out where the guy was, who he was, and how to keep him away from Essie.

"There's something else. Something that I think really scared her and made her feel so violated, and why she's so shy and was hesitant in letting us so close," Max said.

"What else?" Slayer asked through clenched teeth.

Max took a deep breath and then exhaled.

"The guy at some point, maybe when she was in the hospital recovering, got into her apartment and wired it with cameras."

"Oh no," Ford said and ran his palm along his beard.

"He was watching her. Shower, dress, undress, and even sleep. I think it all adds to the anxiety attacks and her panicking," Max told them.

"Motherfucker. We need to find this guy. We need to protect Essie," Cobra stated firmly as he texted.

Turbo walked out of the room and then returned with his laptop. Cobra was texting on his cell phone. Fifteen minutes later, Turbo was turning the computer toward them. The images taking Max's breath away. Photographs from the police file of Essie at the hospital. The room went silent.

"I'll find him and eliminate him," Slayer said. His voice, his tone, hard and cold.

"There'll be no killing of anyone yet, Slayer. We need to be careful. We can help find out who this guy is and where he is. The cops can't find him, so that means he's hiding out. We put out the feelers, send in trackers, and identify and locate. No going off hunting quite yet," Cobra said. Slayer stared at the pictures and then stood up, nearly knocking over the chair.

"Where are you going?" Turbo asked him.

He didn't respond.

"We need to keep her close to us. The only way to do that is to get her to spend time with us as much as possible. To get her here, and to make it so that she isn't alone too often," Turbo said to them.

"We can't take over her life. It will only upset her more and make her keep her distance. We have to be a team," Ford said.

"Tell that to Slayer. I don't know what he's thinking or where he just went, but we have to care for her together, or this isn't going to work," Max said to them, and they all agreed.

* * * *

Essie slipped on a pair of light lounge pants and a tank top after her shower and drying her hair. She felt antsy, nervous, and even her heart was racing. It was like she suddenly dreaded being alone. She thought about Max, Slayer, Ford, Turbo, and Cobra. Was she clinging to something, creating a connection, a need out of fear, or was this real? Was she needing their presence to feel safe?

Tears stung her eyes, and her belly ached. Was she losing her mind finally?

She shook the thoughts from her head and the desires, the need burning in her. She had to evaluate this attraction. It couldn't be this strong so quickly, and it wouldn't be smart. But then she thought about their bodies, their sizes and capabilities, and Max's words today. To trust them to protect her, to not hurt her but to make her their woman. Did she want that?

She was heading into the living room, looking around the small, quiet apartment. No sound could be heard from in here, and suddenly it seemed more like a prison than a home. It was behind the gift shop, closed for the night, and in the back of the building. Perhaps this wasn't such a smart location, but at the time she thought privacy, being hidden from prying eyes would be smartest. Now she wasn't so sure. She started to feel panicked when she heard a knock at her door. She jumped, her heart felt like it was in her throat, and she froze in place, wondering who it could be? She reached for the bat, then gripped her cell phone. She made her way closer to the door. She jumped at the second knock, then peeked through the peephole and gasped. Slayer?

She put the bat down, and then unlocked the two deadbolts and then the regular lock. She opened the door.

"Slayer?" she asked. He stepped toward her, and she moved to the side. She closed the door, and when she turned around, he just stared at her from head to toe. His eyes were narrowed, looking at her, taking in her body, her facial expression, and she couldn't move. She needed him. Had he needed her, too? He reached out and caressed her cheek. She closed her eyes and exhaled.

She wore no bra, and she tried moving her arm, but he gripped her hand. "No. Let me look at you," he said so strong and deeply it made her shiver, and her pussy throbbed. She swallowed hard. She didn't know what was wrong with him. Why was he acting so strangely?

"You're scaring me," she whispered, a tear falling. She was oversensitive, emotional, scared out of her mind tonight and didn't know why. His eyes widened, and then he pulled her into his arms and hugged her tight.

It was instant. That feeling of being protected with a shield of body armor so big, so solid strong that nothing could penetrate it or get to her, but him and his cousins. She knew it instantly. She wanted, needed them. It just happened, and she didn't know if she should deny it or accept it, but she squeezed him back needing all his strength and power that he seemed to possess. That they all seemed to possess. It was irrational thinking, and she didn't care.

"Never be scared of me. I had to see you. To hold you and look at your beautiful face." She realized that Max told him and the others. She squeezed him tight.

"I feel better knowing that you know my secret. Max helped me so much today," she said to him.

He pulled back to look at her. "You're so sweet, so feminine and beautiful. You didn't deserve what that monster did to you. It isn't right that you live in fear, that you kept it all inside and let it eat you alive and into these panic attacks."

Tears spilled from her eyes and his eyes followed them and then her lips then back to her eyes again. He wiped them away with the pad of his thumbs. "I know fear. I know pain, and have had experiences that haunt me every night, too." She squinted at him.

"You do?" He nodded and stroked her lower lip. "Lately, when I have them, I..."

"Slayer?" She waited for him to finish but instead he pressed his lips to hers and kissed her tenderly, deeply, lifted her in his arms and pressed her up against the wall by the front door. She ran her fingers through his hair, and he rocked his hips against hers. When his hand slid under her shirt and against her breast, she moaned into his mouth and her pussy leaked. The feel of his touch, the way his thick, hard thumb brushed over her nipple back and forth did things to her, made her want without care. Could she let go with him and his cousins? The thought of all five extra-large men in size, personalities, and all aspects scared the heck out of her.

He slid his mouth from her lips to her jaw and her neck, then lower. He lifted her top and exhaled.

"So beautiful. My God, Essie, you're incredible." He licked her nipple and then tugged it. She gasped and gripped his wide shoulders and instinctively rocked her hips. Her body knew better than she did what to do, how to react to this man's moves. She needed to slow things down and be rational here. Jumping into bed with five men may not be the wisest move in her life, but it was a hell of a way to lose her virginity. She realized that if she did, she would want to share all of her, and the one thing not tainted or forcefully taken from her, her virginity to them.

She didn't think she was ready. Not yet.

"Slayer. Please, Slayer, we need to slow down. It's too much," she told him and he released her nipple, swirled his tongue over it and then looked at her. He cupped the breast he had feasted on and once again stroked the nipple with the pad of his thumb arousing her all the way to her cunt. She still held on to his shoulders as he stared down into her eyes.

"I'm not leaving you."

"I'm not going to have sex with you. I'm not ready, Slayer. It's…complicated."

"What isn't complicated? I want you. My cousins want you. Spending as much time together as possible is the answer."

"But then I'll want to give in to all of you. I won't stand a chance."

"You'll want to give in because you feel what we feel. Desire, need, a possessiveness and a protectiveness for you." She realized that she felt it for them, too. She was denying these feelings with thoughts of somehow protecting them from Blade, yet not even thinking how stupid that was when she wouldn't be able to protect herself from Blade. She was being possessive of them, protective of them, too.

"Two choices. I call my cousins, and we all squeeze into your bed with you, holding you, protecting you, helping to take away the fears, or you come home with me right now and surprise them, letting them know you want them, too, and that this is real." Her heart started to race again, and her mind thought of all their faces, their personalities, and the moments they all shared thus far.

"I can't have sex with all of you. Not yet."

"You can sleep with us. Let us hold you and feel the protection we can provide."

"For tonight only?"

"For tonight to start." He pressed his lips to hers and then wrapped her in his arms before lowering her to her feet.

"I need to change," she said and started to pull away. He looked her over.

"No, you look gorgeous and comfortable. Just grab what you'll need to wear for tomorrow. Come on," he said and then remained holding her hand, and they walked to her bedroom.

* * * *

They were all sitting down at the kitchen table. It was eleven and still no sign of Slayer. Cobra finally closed up the laptop and stopped staring at the pictures of Essie's battered body, and reading and rereading the medical charts. She could have died by the hands of that fucking monster. He looked at his brothers. Turbo was sitting in the chair in the living room just staring off in deep thought. Ford and Max were still talking strategies of finding the guy and taking him out if the cops didn't do their thing from New York.

When the side door to the kitchen opened, Cobra's eyes widened, and he immediately stood up. There were Slayer and Essie. Her eyes looked teary, and he went to her, flashes of her battered body filled his head, and he pulled her into his arms and hugged her tight. She hugged him back.

He heard his brothers all come in there. Over her shoulder, he looked at Slayer.

"She's staying with us. I didn't give her much of a choice, and explained how we need her as much as she needs us," he said and walked to the refrigerator.

Cobra pulled back, cupped her cheeks, and looked into her eyes.

"I'm glad you're here. We all wanted, needed to see you."

"I know, Cobra. I know Max told you everything."

She looked sad and embarrassed, and it tore at his heart.

"You're so precious, baby. I'm so happy that you're here." He pressed is lips to hers and kissed her, and when her arms wrapped around him and kissed him back, he felt such relief he moaned into her mouth. He lifted her up and placed her on the island. He body felt incredible. She smelled incredible as he released her lips, kept a possessive hand on her neck under the back of her head as he held her gaze.

He heard Ford clear his throat and he smiled. So did she. He released her, and Ford stepped between her legs and gripped her hips.

"Are you okay?"

"I am now," she said and he swallowed down the emotion her words sent through him. He stroked her lower lip.

"I can't even tell you how happy I am that you're here. That I can see you and know that you're safe."

"I appreciate that. Slayer told me that you all would feel a lot better if I was here tonight." He smiled.

"We're a family, we're close, and we all know what we need and want. It's you, Essie. You." Then he pressed his lips to hers. Cobra watched Ford kiss her and Essie hold on to him and run her hands up and down his arms. This was real. It was happening.

* * * *

Turbo stood there with his hands in his pockets watching Essie get kissed and welcomed by his brothers. Max was hugging her, holding her, and she opened her eyes and locked gazes with Turbo, who had yet to greet her. He couldn't stop the images of her battered body from popping into his head. The thoughts of how scared she was, how close she could have come to death, and the fact the guy could have raped her, too. Was that his next plan? Was that why he broke into her apartment and stuck the knife in her pillow? Why hadn't the police been able to find the guy? He knew, as his brothers did, Special Forces guys were the best at evading capture and carrying out missions no matter what the danger or the abilities of those he plans to infiltrate. This man was out there, and he wanted to do harm, perhaps rape and kill Essie.

"Turbo," Cobra said his name and when he refocused he saw Essie staring at him.

"We saw the pictures. We read the files from the hospital, from the police and detectives in New York." Her eyes widened, and she looked at all of them and then covered her mouth with her hand, tears spilling from her eyes. He closed the space between them and cupped her cheeks, pressed her thighs wider, and she held on to his hands.

"He will never get his hands on you as long as we're with you protecting you. Do you understand me, baby? We will protect you from him always. Let us handle things. Let us do what we do best. Let us love you," he said so intensely, and then kissed her mouth, her chin, and then her lips again before he pulled her into his arms and hugged her tight. She hugged him back and cried.

"This is crazy. I want to believe you, but I don't want you to get hurt." She fisted his shirt with her hands. She chuckled and cried at the same time.

"Get hurt?" he asked pulling back. "Honey, take a good fucking look. They don't come any tougher, any harder than the five of us. We're taking care of you and protecting you. You're going to accept it, embrace it, and realize that this is real, and by God, forever," he said and then kissed her again.

That kiss intensified pretty damn quickly, and he lowered her back to the island and made out with her right there in the kitchen with his brothers and cousin looking on. His cock hardened, and his body and heart knew he wanted this petite, sexy little woman to belong to all of them. She was it. The one woman to bring them all together and seal the deal.

As he released her lips and she exhaled, he lifted her top and began to kiss her skin, along that sexy belly ring and tight abs then when he heard her gasp and glanced up to see Slayer gently pull her hands and arms above her head. She locked gazes with him

"Let us bring you pleasure and make you feel good. We need it. To know that you're safe and okay. We won't go too far unless you're ready," he said to her.

Cobra caressed a palm up her belly. She gasped and looked at him.

"So soft and sexy. We stop when you say stop, but don't say it out of fear. Let go, and we'll catch you," he told her, then used one hand to unclip her bra. The second her large, full breasts emerged, Cobra lowered down to feast on one breast as Ford slid over the island to feast on her other breast.

He locked gazes with Slayer who nodded and then kissed Essie from above.

Turbo kissed along the waist of her lounge pants, then lowered them and her panties down and off of her. She tightened up, but Max was there to give her direction.

"Nice and easy, baby. It will feel really good. You'll see," he said, and Turbo inhaled her scent then licked her cunt. She moaned and thrust her hips upward, and it was on. They all began to feast on her body, bringing her pleasure, together. His heart pounded inside of his chest. The fact that he was sharing her with his cousin and brothers made his dick so fucking hard he thought he might explode in his pants. He didn't fucking care. This little lady packed one hell of a fucking punch.

The sight of her on the island in their kitchen with them all surrounding her feasting on her like a midnight snack had him stroking fingers into her cunt and alternating tongue and fingers. She was rocking her hips when Slayer released her lips, and she cried out her release. Turbo slurped and sucked at her cunt until she was pleading for mercy. He felt the slap to his shoulder, and he pulled back, and Max took his place.

"Oh God, please. Please, this is wild," she stated. "This is nothing. Just wait," Cobra said and tugged on her nipple, then kissed her lips. He moved from his position and Turbo took his place. He held her gaze.

"Taste how delicious you are," he said to her and pressed his mouth to hers. He felt her jerk then moan, and he knew that Max was now bringing her pleasure, too.

* * * *

Max slid his palms up and down her thighs spreading her wider. He stroked his tongue along her pussy and then her anus. She wiggled and thrust upward, and he was on fire with the desire to pleasure her. He stroked a finger into her cunt and watched her cream drip. She was so fucking responsive.

"That's it, baby. Give it to me. Come for me next," he said firmly. Turbo released her lips, and she cried out. He stroked her pussy and then felt the tap to his shoulder. Ford wanted in.

"She's so delicious, bro," Max said and moved out of the way and looked at Essie. She was panting, and her eyes glazed over.

"I wouldn't expect anything less from our little lady," Ford told her and then he leaned over her, kissed her belly as Cobra and Slayer cupped her breasts and aroused her nipples. Her hips jerked.

"Oh God, I can't believe this. Is this really happening?" she asked, and her voice cracked.

"Oh yeah, baby. It's happening," Ford said and winked at her. Max chuckled and then moved behind her and caressed her hair.

"You are so very beautiful, baby. Your body knows and responds to each of us. That's perfect." He pressed his lips to hers and then she moaned into his mouth as she jerked upward.

"Fuck, her ass is super fucking tight. God, I'm going to come in my pants." Ford stated, and Max knew he stroked her ass. He released her lips, and Essie cried out her release while Ford fingered both holes.

"This is bad." She shook her head side to side, moaning and thrusting.

"So bad and naughty and, oh God, I never!" she cried out again.

"Fuck, she is coming all over the place. My turn," Cobra stated, and Ford pulled fingers from her body and stepped aside, he immediately went to her and cupped her cheeks.

"You are going to be an amazing lover. We're going to fill you up in every hole and claim you, baby. Nice and easy, and slow, so you can get used to our big, hard cocks," he said and pressed his lips over hers.

Max chuckled. He had never heard Ford carry on so much over a woman and say the things he was saying to Essie. It aroused him, too.

"Mmm," Cobra moaned as he slurped and suckled her cunt and then lifted one of her thighs up over his shoulder. Ford released her lips.

"Cobra!" she yelled.

* * * *

"Damn, we are going to need a lot of lube for this ass. She is fucking tight," he said, stroking a finger into her ass, his mouth wet with her cream. He held her gaze and stroked deeper.

"You like that, baby? Ever have a cock in your ass?" Cobra asked, and she shook her head.

"That's hot. A virgin ass," Ford said and smiled wide.

"I call in first," Cobra said. Then he licked her cunt and suckled against her clit until Slayer gave his shoulder a tap.

He didn't want to stop, but he knew he needed to share. This was only the beginning. They were going to claim her tonight.

He lowered her thigh and Slayer moved in between her legs. Cobra kissed her lips, and she reached up and ran her fingers through his hair. He felt her jerk and then moan.

* * * *

The sights, the sounds, and the intensity of the connection Slayer felt made him desperate to claim Essie with his cousins. This was the feeling, the bond that had been missing all along. That made him stay separate from them and miss his brother, and long for what they could have had. Now, with Essie, anything seemed possible, and the fact that she was in danger, just added to the desire to make her his woman.

"You are so fucking wet, honey. I think your idea of literally just sleeping in our arms isn't going to happen. We're going to claim you tonight. Claim this tight wet pussy and tight, virgin ass." He stroked a finger into her anus, and she cried out.

He saw her grip Cobra's head as he suckled her one breast and Max held her other arm behind her head as Ford suckled her other breast. Cobra stood right by Slayer, and they held her gaze.

"We want you. Let us make love to you. Don't think about any other lovers. Just us from here on out."

Tears rolled down her cheeks, and he narrowed his eyes at her, pulled fingers from her body, and they all stopped and stared at her. Had they hurt her? Scared her?"

"Essie?" Cobra said her name before Slayer could. She shook her head.

She looked at each of them.

As she tried to get up, Max, Ford, and Turbo assisted her. Slayer placed hands on her hips. She looked incredible. She was naked, love bites were scattered along her breasts, her neck, and inner thighs. He wanted to brand her in some way their woman. Claim her like no other men ever had in her life. It was wild, possessive, and barbaric in so many ways.

"There's something I didn't tell you," she whispered. He felt his heart sink to his belly. Was she sexually assaulted? Was she involved with someone else? What the fuck?

He tensed and must have gripped her hips tightly because she placed her hands over his and began to gently stroke his forearms.

"Slayer, ease up please," she whispered, and he did.

"What didn't you tell us?" Cobra demanded in that tone that was all commander.

She looked at him. Then she released one of Slayer's arms and tried covering her breasts.

Max shook his head.

"Uncover yourself. You're perfect, and you're ours."

"I'm the only one naked," she replied.

"We can change that in a flash," Ford said and whipped off his shirt and then started to undo the button on his jeans.

"Wait," she said and reached out and touched his arm, then she reached up and stroked his cheek. Slayer watched Ford's eyes widened, and his cheeks turned red. Essie had the same effect on all of them.

"Another reason why I was resistant to getting involved with all of you, with a ménage relationship was because of your much greater experiences."

"Baby, you will benefit completely from our experiences," Cobra said to her firmly and as if she was clueless. Essie lowered her eyes and worried her bottom lip. Turbo cleared his throat.

"Forget about your other lovers. They were nothing compared to us and what we'll be to you," he told her.

She looked at him.

"Um, well, I can't believe I'm sitting on the island in your kitchen naked, that I allowed all five of you to feast on me like some midnight snack, and that I'm baring my soul to you. Now I have to tell you this."

"Just tell us. Whatever it is, we'll handle it together," Max said to her. She slightly chuckled.

Now Slayer was growing impatient.

"Say it. Just spit it the fuck out," Slayer stated, and her eyes widened, and she held his gaze. She ran her hands up his forearms again and then gripped them.

"What we did on this island, I never allowed any man to ever do to me. No man, not ever, has kissed me, touched me, in the places that you and your cousins have touched me. There are no other lovers to compare you to. No other men I've trusted enough to let into my body. It's the only thing I have left to give of me that hasn't been taken against my will. So, I'm scared, I'm hesitant, I'm—"

"A virgin?" Ford interrupted.

"Whoa," Turbo whispered.

"Jesus," Cobra said.

"We hit the fucking jackpot," Max stated, and she chuckled, and so did they. Slayer reached up and cupped her cheek.

"No one ever, baby? You're a virgin, never had sex ever?" he asked.

She shook her head.

He pressed his lips to hers and kissed her, then lifted her up into his arms and carried her from the kitchen.

* * * *

Essie didn't know what Slayer was going to do, but she was relieved to get this out. To take the chance and tell them the truth. What they shared in the kitchen was amazing, and suddenly nothing else mattered but having them, claiming them, and being claimed by them and praying that it wasn't a huge mistake or she was screwed. What man would want her after being the lover to five men? When she thought that, it didn't seem possible that there would be any other men in her life that she would want like these five men. That she could feel comfortable and safe with. Could they protect her from Blade? Did she want them to? Wasn't that asking for them to get hurt or possibly get in trouble with the law? She was so scared, and she wouldn't stand a chance against Blade a second time.

Essie felt Slayer lower her to the bed. She gripped his shoulders.

"I'm going to get undressed and just hold you. When you're ready, whether it's tonight or some other night, we'll make love to you together, and we'll seal this connection forever," he said and kissed her forehead. She saw the others filter into the room and start getting undressed.

"Forever?" she asked.

"Honey, I'm thirty-fucking-six-years-old. I know I got some years, some wear and tear, and can be difficult to get along with, but I know one fucking thing for certain. I'm not ever going to let you go. This is the real fucking deal. When you can accept that and are willing to accept all of us, that's when we'll make love to you and claim you our woman." He removed everything, and stood before her naked, with a thick, long cock tapping his belly. She swallowed hard, wondering how that could fit inside of her and hoping that it would feel even better than his fingers. It had to, and the deeper it went, the more electrifying it would feel. He slid behind her, pulled her into his arms, that thick, hard cock tapping against her ass and back, and then Cobra slid onto the bed. Naked and just as big, thick, and hard. He snuggled close and placed a hand on her hip then stroked her breast.

"Just feel us surrounding you, keeping you safe, and know that it will only get stronger and better," Cobra said and then pressed his lips to hers, and she was overwhelmed with emotions. She slid her arms around his neck and pushed him to his back. Slayer released her, and she climbed on top of Cobra and gave her all in that kiss. She absorbed the feel of his cock against her belly and his palms smoothing over her ass, spreading her thighs, then stroking her cunt. She lifted up and pulled from his mouth, and he suckled a breast.

"Oh, Cobra. I want all of you. I want to take this chance despite my fears. I want to feel more of what I felt downstairs," she admitted, and he tugged hard on her breast making her gasp.

She held his gaze, his dark blue eyes bore into hers, and the feel of his large hand squeezing her ass tight gave him her full attention.

"There will be no turning back after we make love to you together. No holding back, no regrets, and there will be rules to follow as our woman. Do you accept that and understand it?" he asked firmly. Like some commanding military man, her gut instincts understood it all, and she accepted it. She knew this was right and she wanted nothing more than for them to belong to her, too.

"You'll be all mine. All of you. No other women but me," she stated. She didn't ask.

He winked.

"Only you and something tells me, you're going to be a handful," he said and then kissed her again, rolled her to her back, and spread her thighs with his own.

She ran her hands along his hair and over his shoulders. He stroked her cunt immediately, and she moaned. When Cobra released her lips, they locked gazes.

"Do we need condoms?" he asked.

"I'm on the pill," she said to him.

He smiled.

"Good. No fucking barriers, and you relax and let us all make love to you. Later, once we get your body adjusted, we'll take you together. Understood?" He was so damn authoritative. Her cheeks warmed and her pussy clenched.

"Yes, sir," she said, then heard the chuckles.

"Definitely going to be a handful," he said and added a second digit to her count, making her grip his shoulders and cry out a moan.

She felt her hands being raised above her head and then her thighs spread wider.

Max slapped his hands together as Slayer held her arms above her head and started to feast on her breast.

"Where to begin," Max teased and then lowered down to suckle her other breast.

She shook her head side to side, shocked at what their mouths, their words did to her.

Cobra spread her thighs and pulled fingers from her cunt and began to suckle her clit then stroke his tongue back and forth over her pussy and anus. She shivered and moaned.

"Oh, please, Cobra, please," she begged.

"Take her, commander. Lead the way, and we'll follow so we have one another's backs," Ford said as he and Turbo stood there naked, stroking their cocks and watching.

She moaned from the sight, and Cobra lifted up.

"Together, one after the next, so we claim her virginity together," he said. He aligned his cock with her pussy and held her gaze.

"Accept us?" he asked.

"Yes, Cobra. All of you. Please," she said and could feel this strong, magical kind of sensation surround all of them.

She saw Ford and Turbo step back. They took positions on either side of Cobra and Slayer, as well as Max.

She locked gazes with Cobra and felt the tip of his cock begin to push into her tight cunt.

He clenched his teeth, looking so sexy and in control.

Slayer and Max both took that moment to suck on her tits hard then tug on both nipples. She lifted her pelvis and cried out as Cobra thrust into her to the hilt.

"Fuck," he moaned, gripping her hips and holding himself still deep inside her.

"Holy fucking shit, baby. So tight. Jesus," Cobra exclaimed and slightly pulled out, then slowly pushed into her.

"Fuck," he moaned and clenched his teeth, turning red, and she saw the veins by the side of his temples pulsate.

She gasped on every deep stroke but felt like he was holding back, or trying to go slow, and she knew she needed fast.

"Take me, Cobra. Faster, please," she demanded.

"Do it. We got you, and she needs it like this. Do it," Slayer stated, and Cobra began to set a fast, steady pace. In and out, he thrust his thick, hard cock into her sensitive pussy, making her moan and cream more and more. As he started to grunt and curse about how tight she was and not wanting to come yet, she felt her inner core tighten, and the something overwhelmed her even greater than when they fingered her on the kitchen island.

"Cobra, oh God, Cobra." She gasped and her breath caught in her throat as the orgasm struck her hard and she cried out.

"Fuck," he yelled, then thrust into her harder, faster, nonstop. Max and Slayer stepped aside, and Cobra grabbed her hips, then cupped her breasts before grasping her shoulders, rocking into her deeply.

"Mine. Mine," he stated so possessively, and she exhaled in pleasure and felt him come inside of her. He wrapped his arms around her, nearly crushing her to him, and rolled to his side, ran his hand over her ass. He cupped the ass cheek, then her back as he kissed her lips, neck, and her breast before making his way back up to her lips again.

"Tell me I didn't hurt you."

"You didn't," she said and squeezed him tight.

* * * *

Max slid in behind Essie. Cobra smiled and caressed her cheek.

"Max needs you," he told her, then pressed his lips to hers and slowly moved away.

Max inhaled her shampoo and snuggled against her back. He trailed kisses along her shoulders and held her close. He couldn't believe how good it felt to have her in his arms, skin-to-skin, knowing he was about to claim her next.

He trailed kisses along her neck and shoulder, then rolled her to her back, and kissed her on the mouth while easing his thick, hard thigh between her legs. He held himself upright on his forearms, devouring her moans, absorbing the feeling of being this close to her. When their lips parted, he eased her thighs opened, held her gaze, and waited a moment.

"Are you ready for me?" he asked her and stroked her hair and cheeks.

"Yes, Max."

He absorbed the dark blue of her eyes, the softness of her skin, the feel of her underneath him, legs spread, his cock at her warm pussy, and he licked his lips.

"You're a dream, Essie. You already mean so much to me, baby, and I promise to protect you always."

Her lips parted. She held on to his waist as she began to nudge his cock into her cunt.

She slid her hands up and down his waist and held tight.

"I promise to protect you, too, Max," she said, and he felt his gut clench and a feeling of fear, of need to possess her fully overtake all other thoughts as he slid the rest of the way into her tight, wet cunt.

They both sighed and he held himself in place while he cupped her cheeks, kissed the corner of her mouth, then her jaw, then back to her mouth. As he pulled back, she followed, lifting her head as if she didn't want his kisses to stop.

"Now I claim you as my woman, too," he said.

Max eased her arms up above her head.

"Max." She exhaled.

He stared down into her eyes, pulled back, and then thrust into her. He was lost in her body, in the sounds of the soft moans that filled her air.

"My God, woman, you are tight," he said and pulled back, clenched his teeth, then thrust back in.

"Faster, Max. Please move faster. It's torture," she said and rolled her head side to side.

He gripped her hips and gave her what she wanted. What she said she needed, and he let himself go. He knew his brothers and Slayer watched over them, and it gave him peace of mind and a feeling of security he didn't realize aroused him to another level until this moment when they shared Essie as one.

Over and over, he thrust his hips and grunted, then came, filling her with his seed and knowing it was only the beginning of his claim of her.

He released her arms, and she hugged him to her chest. She clung to him, kissed his neck and shoulder, and then remained holding him until Ford cleared his throat.

* * * *

Max slid from her body and Ford approached with a washcloth to clean her up and then dry her off. He slid over her and then pulled her into his arms and kissed her tenderly along her lips, her jaw, and throat.

"My God, you're so petite and sexy. This body is exceptional, and after tonight, you'll belong to all of us, forever," he said and then pulled her against his chest.

Ford lay on his back, and Essie lifted up and ran her fingers along his bare chest. It tickled, and he gripped her hand. He released it without a word, and she lifted up and kissed his lips.

She played with his beard and then lifted up and let the whiskers rub over her breasts.

"Does that feel good, baby?" he asked her.

"Yes," she said, and he pulled one of her thighs up over his hip, then slid a finger into her cunt.

Ford watched her close her eyes, then rock her hips against his body. She was instantly wet—he felt it against his skin.

"Sweet, sweet Essie," he whispered and then lifted her up higher so he could suckle her breast and use his beard to tickle her skin like she seemed to like.

She held on to his shoulders and rocked her hips against his fingers.

"Fuck. I need in," he growled, lost the ability to go slow and rolled her to her back, spread her thighs, and thrust into her fully.

She gasped, grabbed on to his shoulders and he was lost inside of her.

He didn't have a care in the world but to claim Essie his woman along with his brothers, his cousin, his family.

In and out, he stroked her cunt harder, faster. He gripped her hips, lifted them up, and pounded into her cunt.

"Ford. Oh God, Ford." She cried out. Her dark blue eyes appeared glazed over, and those luscious lips he dreamt about kissing, possessing turned him on even further.

"You're so fucking sexy and beautiful. I've wanted to get lost inside of you for so long, Essie, and now you're mine."

"Yes, Ford, oh God, yes. Yes," she moaned and then she gasped and came.

He felt her pussy explode and that was it for Ford. He thrust and stroked until he could no longer hold back as he claimed her his woman and came.

* * * *

Essie was trying to catch her breath. She also couldn't help but to reach out and caress Ford's shoulders and all those muscles as he kissed her everywhere his lips could go. Her heart hammered inside of her chest, and she rolled to her belly as Ford massaged her muscles. She felt the bed dip and then the second set of hands landed on her thighs and began to massage upward.

Ford whispered into her ear.

"Let Turbo claim you his woman next, sweetie." He kissed her shoulder, and she looked back at Turbo, then closed her eyes and moaned.

He eased up over her, straddled her body, and began to massage her shoulders and down her arms. His hands and fingers were thick and hard but felt incredible kneading her muscles. When he used his thumbs to stroke against her ass cheeks, hitting sensitive spots along the way that aroused her, she couldn't stop the moan from escaping her mouth.

"Oh yeah, someone likes a massage," he whispered next to her neck and ear then kissed her skin. She could feel his thick, long cock stroke over the crack of her ass and she moaned again.

"Such a sexy body. My lord, honey, this ass is fucking perfect." He used his thumbs to stroke her open as he lifted up and fingers slid from her crack, over her anus, to her very wet pussy.

"Turbo," she moaned and began to thrust against his fingers as they slid into her channel.

"Lift those hips and ass. Show me what it's going to look like when we fuck this ass later tonight," he said, his dirty talk arousing her.

"Holy damn, bro," Max said aloud, and she moaned and lifted her hips upward.

"Fuck," Turbo said loudly, shocking her. Then she felt him lift her hips, climb up between her legs, and use his cock to stroke against her pussy and her ass.

"Turbo," she stated.

"Oh yeah, baby. I'm going to fuck this sweet, tight pussy from behind while I play with this sexy ass and get it ready for cock."

Smack.

"Oh God."

Smack.

"Oh." She moaned at the sensations as Turbo smacked her ass, shocking her. She felt the sting, wasn't sure how she felt about it, but then he shoved into her cunt from behind, filling her with his cock as the sensations were still present from the spanking.

"Turbo." She gripped the comforter, held her position on all fours, and took whatever Turbo wanted to give her. In a flash, she was begging for more.

"Oh, Turbo. Turbo, please, I need more." She exclaimed and then she felt something thick and cold against her anus, then something fell to the bed.

She glanced that way as Turbo stroked his cock into her pussy from behind to find Cobra there. He dropped a tube of something onto the bed and then—

"Oh God," she exclaimed as the cool liquid along with his thick, hard finger slid into her anus.

Her body instantly erupted, and she cried out, rocking her hips back against Turbo's cock as she came.

"Oh yeah, our woman is going to love getting fucked in the ass. Fuck yeah," he carried on.

"Holy shit," Ford exclaimed and then climbed up on the bed and caressed her hair down to her back. She couldn't even comprehend what was happening. She loved the sensations, craved feeling more and more, and then Turbo grunted and came. He shook behind her, pulled his fingers from her ass making her shiver, and then hugged and kissed her everywhere.

"Get over here, Slayer, and claim our woman so we can take her together," he said.

He eased out, and she lifted up only for Slayer to pull her into his arms and hold her against his chest. He rolled her onto her back and stared down into her eyes.

"Are you okay?" he asked and looked at her closely as if he would notice if she weren't okay. He was so caring and loving.

"Take me, Slayer. Now. Do it please so we're all one," she said to him.

He lifted up and looked around him. She couldn't understand why, and a moment later, he slid into her channel and closed his eyes.

"Holy God."

"Yes, Slayer. Oh yes," she said and gripped his shoulders, lifting up to kiss his chin.

He tilted down and stared at her.

"Heaven. You're heaven," he said and began to stroke into her pussy. Back and forth, he lifted up and thrust his thick, hard cock into her cunt. He went slow, torturing her, looking around at his brothers then back at her. He suddenly seemed hesitant.

"Slayer," she said his name and he looked down into her eyes.

"Let go. Take me. Claim me and let go like you asked me to," she said to him. He swallowed hard again, and she looked at his body, saw the red mark on his side like some scar, and she ran her hands up over it. He gripped her hands, pushed them above her head, and stared down into her eyes.

Cobra was on one side and Turbo on the other.

"We got your six. Claim our woman. She belongs to all of us, now," Cobra ordered.

She wasn't sure what was happening, but in that moment, Slayer seemed to release a sigh and then opened his eyes and looked possessive. It was wild, and both scared her and aroused her. Her pussy erupted.

"Mine. You're mine." He slid his hands up from her wrists to her shoulders and began to thrust and rock into her cunt. Faster, deeper he hammered into her pussy, and she cried out her release and came.

"Together, brothers. Together," he stated and rolled to his back taking her with him. He gripped her face and head.

"You belong to us now, Essie. We will protect you always." He pulled her down to kiss him, and she felt him wiggle down the bed with her on top of him, still deep in her cunt. When she felt the second set of hands on her hips running up and down her back, she knew their intention, and she wanted it. She felt the desperation Slayer emitted. When he released her lips, she lifted up.

"Teach me how," she said to him and he gripped her hips, narrowed his eyes, and thrust up into her.

"Move those sexy hips. Ride my cock, claim me as your man. Just feel it, baby, while Ford gets ready to fill that ass with cock." Max returned from the bathroom wiping down his cock with a towel, but her focus went back to riding Slayer.

She rocked her hips, closed her eyes, and began to get a feel for being on top.

He cupped her breasts and pulled on the nipples.

"Slayer."

"Fuck me, woman. Claim me yours," he ordered.

"Oh God." She jerked and then moaned and lowered against Slayer.

"That's it, woman. Feel my fingers and the lube stretching this ass. We have big cocks, and you're so tight, our little virgin," Ford stated and eased fingers in and out of her ass.

"Oh, Ford. Oh God, yes. I want it," she said as the burning subsided and then she felt the hand against her cheek. Max was there holding his cock in his hand.

"I need that sexy mouth. We need to take you together," Max said.

"I never…"

"That's fucking hot. Jesus, we really did hit the fucking jackpot," he said and eased her head toward his cock.

She was nervous but so aroused surrounded by all these muscles and the orders and tone. It was military sexy, and she suddenly wanted to please all of them and prove that she wasn't weak or so fragile. There was no fear to her when the danger that lay beyond their doors and then fear of losing them. She licked along the tip of Max's cock and then opened for him to slide into her mouth. At the same time, he moaned, Ford slid finger out of her ass and replaced them with his cock.

"Here I come, sexy," he said and eased the thick, bulbous top into the tight rings. She gasped and moaned as Slayer thrust upward and held himself deep.

Smack.

Smack.

She moaned, and Ford eased the rest of the way into her ass, and they all moaned together.

That was it. It turned into complete chaos, and she let go and allowed them to take everything and anything they wanted.

"Holy God, Essie. My God, woman," Ford exclaimed and fucked her ass, thrusting and stroking until he couldn't move. He hollered about her being a fucking goddess and came in her ass. She moaned and sucked harder on Max, who shot his seed down her throat.

Just as Ford eased out and she felt the loss, strong, hard hands gripped her hips and more lube was pushed into her ass.

"Mine," Turbo said and then slid into her ass without hesitation.

Max pulled from her mouth, and Cobra took his place. She accepted him immediately, and all three men moved in sync. She sucked and moaned until Turbo came and then Cobra followed. The moment they pulled away, Slayer rolled her to the side and then to her back and thrust so fast and deep she lost her breath and screamed until her voice was hoarse.

"Ours forever. You feel like home, Essie. Home," Slayer exclaimed and then came.

Chapter Seven

Essie walked through the darkness. There wasn't a sound, and it was so eerie she hesitated to go further, closer to her parent's house. She had to see them. She missed them so much. She'd tried calling and hadn't gotten an answer. She was so worried. She approached with caution, still not seeing anything out of the ordinary. Their car was in the driveway. A light was on in the living room. She longed to feel their arms around her. To hear their voices and to be with them. The need was so great she felt tightness everywhere.

She slowly opened the door, surprised that it was unlocked. It creaked open, and she pushed it the rest of the way. Her eyes widened, and she nearly tumbled backward at the sight of all the blood. Her parents lay there on the rug and Blade stood over them.

"Welcome home, Essie," he stated smirking and holding the bloody knife in his hand.

She screamed and cried out, then tried to run for her life, but her feet were stuck, as if they were cemented to the ground and Blade tackled her to the ground, the hit so hard, his body so heavy, she couldn't breathe. She wasn't breathing.

She grabbed her neck, reached out and felt something, and kept grabbing and gasping. She was going to die.

"Essie! Wake the fuck up now!"

She jerked forward.

A nightmare? It was a nightmare. It wasn't real. She scanned around her. She grabbed her throat and gasped for breath that wasn't coming. Her heart was racing, she was in a full-fledged panic attack and Max, Ford, Turbo, Cobra, and Slayer were surrounding her.

"Here, here." Slayer brought her the paper bag. She grabbed it from him, crumpled it, and slid to the floor by the bed. She took in the steady breaths and tried not to focus on how embarrassing this was, and instead on what the doctor explained she should do. Easy breaths. Nice, easy breaths.

"Slowly, Essie. Slowly, baby, you're safe. It was a nightmare," Slayer said to her and caressed the hair from her damp cheeks. She closed her eyes, willed the fear the images from the nightmare away, and slowly started to settle down. She pulled the bag from her mouth, let her arms hang by her sides, and kept her head back against the bed as she sat there on the rug.

He caressed her hair from her cheeks.

"What do you need? What helps?" Slayer asked her.

"Water. Protein bar, something," she whispered and sensed them moving, but she was utterly exhausted.

"Should we put her on the bed?" Cobra asked. She shook her head slowly.

"Jesus, baby. This happens every day?" Ford asked her. She kept her eyes closed.

"Yes."

"Here. I got the water and a protein bar," Turbo said, and Slayer lifted her head. She opened her eyes and locked gazes with his fierce blue ones. She took a sip from the water bottle, then another.

"Want to hold it or just get pieces?" Turbo asked. They were all so caring, but she felt like an invalid, like a crazy, weak idiot. Tears rolled down her cheeks.

"Don't. Don't you dare start those crazy thoughts or feel embarrassed that we're witnessing this. We're a family now. You're our woman, and we are going to protect you with everything we've got," Slayer stated firmly.

She reached out for the bar with a shaking hand. Turbo put the bar into her hand but didn't release her hand. Instead, he helped her to take a bite. The minutes passed as she chewed, then drank, then chewed some more until her body started to get back to feeling normal. Or at least functional.

She looked at all of them. They were surrounding her, staring at her with concern and anger. "I'm sorry."

"No. There isn't anything to be sorry about, Essie," Cobra stated firmly.

"You're angry now. The night is ruined."

"It isn't ruined, baby. If anything, this just makes me want to be with you, protecting you, helping you to heal even more so," Max said to her and caressed her thigh. She realized she was only wearing a T-shirt. Not hers, and she ran her hand along it then gripped Max's hand. "I didn't want you to see me like this. I can't gain any control when it's happening," she said and sniffled.

Ford reached out and wiped away her tears.

"It's brought on by nightmares from the attack?" he asked, and she shook her head.

"Not always. It's always about him. About Blade finding me, or hurting those I love and care about." She closed her eyes and thought about her parents. She shouldn't call them. She shouldn't take the chance that Blade could be watching them, or maybe wired their house or something.

"Hey, what are you thinking about?" Cobra asked. Her heart ached as she realized the consequences of her making love to these men and accepting them as her lovers. Blade could go after each of them, and her parents, and her aunt and uncle, and even Helen. Anyone close to her in order to get to her. She needed to make them all aware of the potential danger. It would be the only way to give them a fighting chance.

"Essie, talk to us. Stop thinking that you're alone. You aren't anymore. You have all of us," Ford stated.

"And if I get you and your brothers, your cousin, Helen, killed, then what?" she asked.

"That isn't going to happen because we know what is going on and will take the proper precautions. Helen will be made aware of the potential danger," Slayer told her.

"She knows I had something bad happen to me in New York. She's friends with my aunt and uncle."

"Your aunt and uncle? Where do they live?" Cobra asked.

"Less than an hour from here. I met Helen and saw the sign for the apartment for rent by coincidence, and when I gave my name, and she knew my aunt and uncle, it just felt right."

"Of course it did, because coming here was the best decision. Now where are your parents? You didn't mention them before," Turbo asked.

"They live in New York. I didn't stay near them in order to protect them. I only get to talk to them every other week or maybe three weeks. I use a burner phone and call a cell phone my dad had a friend set up under the friend's name as precaution so Blade can't track it or me."

"Shit, how the heck did you know how to do that?" Max asked and smiled.

"The movies," she said, and they chuckled. Slayer caressed her thigh.

"We'll need to know where your parents live so we can arrange protection for them," he said.

"What?"

"Baby, you're scared they could get killed by Blade or hurt by him to get to you. They need protection, as do your aunt, uncle, Helen, and whomever else you think may be in harm's way. We told you that we're resourceful and have connections. It wasn't to just get you into bed," Slayer said, making a joke, which was so out of character for him, even his brothers looked shocked.

She tilted her head at him.

"Cute, Slayer," She told him and he cupped her cheek and held her gaze with a firm expression.

"You are our woman and we would give our lives to protect you." Tears spilled from her eyes.

"I don't want you to give your lives to protect me," she said and sniffled.

"The only life that is going to be lost will be Blade's. I promise you," he said and then pressed his lips to hers. When he pulled back, she swallowed hard.

As they began to get up, Slayer went to help lift her, and she shook her head.

"No. I'm upset enough that this happened and you all saw me like this. I'm not a baby who needs to be pacified." She went to push up from the rug, feeling how lightheaded she still was and weak, damn it. She knew it always took her about thirty minutes to recover.

Cobra lowered down and stared into her eyes. "You are not weak, and we do not pacify anyone. We can see how exhausted you are from the episode and it's our responsibility, and pleasure, to take care of our woman. The sooner you realize that you are no longer alone and have all five of us to care for you, the better off you'll be," he stated firmly.

"And the less punishments you'll get," Ford added, standing there glaring at her with his arms crossed in front of his chest.

"Punishments?" she asked as Cobra lifted her up and hugged her close.

"Yes. We'll go over the rules, don't worry," Ford told her with an expression of promise and severity in his eyes. Should she be scared or aroused? She really didn't know, and as Cobra laid her on the bed and held her against his chest, she closed her eyes and rested, thinking if this was real, maybe she would have a fighting chance.

Chapter Eight

"Say that again, Walt," Stewart asked his cousin. He sat forward on the couch and listened to what his cousin said.

"Essie was attacked one night walking home from work. She was beaten badly. Wound up in the hospital for three weeks."

"Holy God," Stewart said and ran his fingers through his hair.

"She wasn't raped, but the reports say that she had a suspicion of who the guy was. Some soldier she met one night with friends, and she never accepted his advances. Never dated him or went out with him, and he basically started stalking her. Her car was broken into and her apartment, too."

"Sounds like a fucking asshole," Stewart said and looked at himself in the mirror. He flexed his muscles. He was a big guy, strong, and even took a bunch of boxing classes.

"This is why she's scared to date. Did the cops catch the guy?"

"No. I don't have any other information. It's pretty obvious she moved out there to South Carolina to hide."

"No shit, Walt. This just pisses me off. I can protect her from this guy. I just need to prove it to her somehow."

"Yeah, well, this guy is a soldier, and he sounds like a psycho. It may be better to just stay out of it."

"She's too beautiful, man."

"I saw a picture of her. She looks really sweet."

"She's going to be mine. I just need to prove to her that I can protect her."

"Whatever, Stewart. No more favors, though. I took a chance looking this shit up. I feel like someone is watching me or I'm going to get busted."

Stewart chuckled. "I appreciate the help. Talk to you soon."

* * * *

Walt disconnected the call and then looked around him. He hated doing this kind of shit. He had a feeling that this situation with this woman was going to get his cousin into some serious trouble. He stood up, grabbed his blazer, and headed out of the office. He didn't like the feeling he had, and when he got into the elevator right before it closed, some guy, a detective or someone he hardly knew but recognized from the department, slid in.

He stared at Walt and Walt gave a nod then looked away.

"Not for nothing, buddy, but you're butting your nose into a serious police investigation. Who the fuck were you giving information to?" the guy asked him.

"What? I don't know what you're talking about," Stewart said, and a second later, he was pressed up against the wall.

"You dumb fuck. We're trying to keep Essie safe. Who were you talking to on the phone about her case?"

Steward felt like throwing up. He was fucked.

"My cousin. He knows her, and he was worried about her and the way she seems like she's hiding out."

The guy narrowed his eyes at him.

"Where does your cousin live?"

"South Carolina."

"That's where he met Essie?"

Stewart nodded, and the guy exhaled.

"Where in South Carolina?" Stewart scrunched his eyes together.

"If you're part of the investigation, why don't you know?" he asked. The guy pressed him harder against the wall. He saw his nameplate. *Kessler*.

"She was super scared and the last detectives working the case weren't exactly giving her the right advice. They screwed up, kind of like you did snooping around the computer system and giving out personal information on Essie and placing her in further danger."

"No, I didn't. I just told my cousin because he likes her and she's shy and not accepting dates from anyone. He isn't going to hurt her, he wants to protect her."

"The name of the town and your cousin's name. Then we'll talk about consequences."

* * * *

Slayer, Ford, and Max walked out of the bedroom giving Essie time to recover and also some time with Cobra and Turbo.

Max watched Slayer texting on his cell phone before going over to the laptop where he began typing.

"Something is up," Max whispered to Ford. Ford rubbed his beard and took a seat by the island along with Slayer.

"You got something?" he asked Slayer.

Max clenched his teeth.

He didn't look up. "Give me a minute," he said and then typed faster, texted, and then stopped, leaned forward, and fixated on the screen.

"What is it? Talk to us, Slayer, we're all in this together," Max said to him.

He leaned back in the chair, his expression grim, angry, and he turned the laptop toward them. Max took position next to Ford.

"Blade, AKA Corey Flint, wanted by the NYPD for assault, several counts, attempted murder, Jesus, it says he assaulted a bunch of residents and the landlord at his apartment complex. One is in critical condition."

Max gripped the counter.

"This is him? This is the fucking asshole?" Ford stated and stared at the screen.

"Dishonorable discharge," Slayer stated and then clicked the button and brought up another screen. Max immediately knew it was a government file. He read the details and the abilities of this man who was after their woman. Who hurt Essie once and now was obsessed with finding her."

"Holy fucking shit," Max stated.

Ford looked toward the bedroom, then stood up and paced.

"No fucking self-defense class is going to help her against a man with these capabilities, Slayer. If he gets his hands on her," Ford stated.

"He won't get his hands on her. We won't let him get close enough."

"But no one has come up with a location on him. We need to find him," Max said, and he felt like a caged animal. Like he needed to go out and hunt this beast down and kill him.

"Don't let on to any of this. We'll talk to Cobra and Turbo later. The only concrete plan would be to call in a few favors, and then I leave and go hunting."

"She is not going to want you to leave here," Max stated.

"She doesn't have a choice. We spend the next week going over the rules of being our woman. She would need to learn them anyway if I decide to take up any of the upcoming assignments," Slayer told them.

"You would still consider being active duty, taking on such dangerous missions with Essie in your life now?" Ford asked him.

"I haven't made any decisions yet. A lot of things happened the last few missions."

"Yeah, like a stab wound that you just happened to not mention," Ford said, reminding him of the damage to his skin and how they didn't say a word in front of Essie, but he saw their pissed expressions.

"It was a minor injury, nothing worth discussing."

"So you say, Slayer, but the one thing you keep forgetting is that it means something to us. We worry about you. You're family, you're more like our brother, and when you hurt, when you're scared or upset, so are we. Having taken Essie together, possessing her together, means things need to change," Ford said to him.

Slayer looked away.

"Our first priority is to eliminate the threat against Essie. Anything else is minimal as far as I'm concerned. Now let me take care of some phone calls and get more intel," Slayer said to them.

"What about Essie, and who's going to protect her?" Max asked.

"You two join the others. I'll take care of this first." He started to type away on the computer and Max looked at Ford who nodded toward the hallway.

"Let's go. He needs to do this and handle it his way," Ford said to Max.

"Doesn't he feel the connection to Essie like we do? I mean, isn't it just as strong for him as it seems to be for us?" Max asked.

"It may be even stronger, but Slayer needs to admit to himself that he loves her, and accept that before he'll let his guard down and accept all that comes along with sharing her. Come on. I need to see her and know that she's safe and all ours."

* * * *

"Cobra. Oh God, Cobra," Essie whispered as Cobra suckled hard on her clit and then plunged his tongue into her channel. Turbo held her arms above her head, and feasted and teased her breasts.

She watched Turbo's tongue lick the tip and then swirl over it before he suckled hard. When he released her nipple, Cobra sat up and gripped her hips.

"We need inside of you, right fucking now."

"Yes," she said, and he moved back. Turbo lifted her up into his arms, scooted down lower on the bed, and then she felt his cock under her pussy and ass.

"Take me inside of you now," Turbo ordered.

She gasped with Cobra's help lifting her up, and she gripped Turbo's cock. He grunted, and she slid her pussy over the hard, thick muscle.

"Good girl," Cobra whispered against her ear, his hands still gripping her hips from behind and pushing down, so she took Turbo in deeply.

"Oh God," she moaned and fell forward only for Turbo to now grip her hips and thrust upward.

How the hell did he do that, have the muscle strength and stamina to thrust upward like that? My God, he was filled with muscles, she thought, gripping his shoulders and rubbing her hand all over Turbo. His abs were super tight and hard, his shoulders wide and that dark hair, those dark eyes bore into hers.

"Mine," he said and thrust upward again.

She felt the cool liquid to her ass.

"There are rules we are going to inform you about along the way," Cobra said to her and then suckle her earlobe.

"Oh, yes, whatever you want, Cobra." She exhaled and felt her pussy leak more cream. Turbo chuckled.

"Whatever we want huh?" he asked and thrust again, then cupped her breasts and tugged hard on her nipples.

She gasped.

Essie felt Cobra's hands slide along her ass and the press of lube to her anus.

"You belong to all of us. When we give an order, you respond immediately. Understood?" Cobra asked and pressed fingers to her anus.

"Understood?" Turbo asked in a firm tone and thrust upward.

"Yes. Oh," she moaned and counterthrust against Turbo's cock, and then shifted back against Cobra's fingers.

Cobra gripped her shoulder, his hand felt so big, solid as he pushed his fingers in and out of her ass.

"That's right, baby, and you know what? We belong to you just as much as you belong to us. You tell us when you need something. When you crave something." He sucked her earlobe into his mouth then blew warm breath into her ear giving her the chills and making her moan louder and thrust faster.

"Give us all of you. Don't hold back. No shields, no hiding from us, ever." He pulled his fingers from her ass, slid in behind her, and thrust his cock into her anus.

She moaned aloud, and he gripped her hips and counterthrust to Turbo's deep strokes.

Cobra's tone, his commanding ways had such an effect on her. She felt wild, needy, and also willing to give them everything, anything they wanted.

"Harder, Cobra, Turbo. Harder," she yelled out and grabbed on to Turbo's shoulders. She rode his cock as best she could with Cobra hammering into her ass.

They were all moaning, and then Cobra grunted aloud. "Come for us." Turbo came, and she continued to thrust and thrust, not yet coming, and feeling desperate.

"Let go," Cobra ordered.

"Please, oh God, please," she begged.

"Give it to her," Turbo stated.

"We're here," Ford and Max said, and Cobra lifted her up by her hips and laid her on all fours on the bed. He continued to thrust into her ass, and she reached below and stroked her own pussy.

"I need you," Max said, and he gripped her hair, and she spotted his cock and opened immediately for him. She sucked on his cock harder than she meant to.

"Jesus, Essie, slow down, baby. Fuck," he complained and then moaned. She sucked harder, bobbed her head up and down.

Smack.

Smack.

"Let go and come. Come when we tell you to come," Cobra said, and she felt her body about to explode in pleasure when Ford pulled on her nipples as he lay on the side of the bed.

"Oh!" she exclaimed and came. She felt her whole body erupt and then Cobra followed and rocked his hips several times before he pulled out.

Max pulled from her mouth and quickly slid underneath her.

"Ride me," he ordered next, and she was still recovering from her orgasm, but she slid over his cock, her pussy so sensitive she kept moaning and gasping.

Smack.

Smack.

"You can take it. You were always meant for us," Ford said.

She felt the cool liquid to her anus and knew he would take her ass next. She wanted it. Craved it when suddenly she felt the bulbous tip to her anus and then Ford slid right in.

"Heaven. You're fucking heaven, Essie," Ford said.

He and Max began a wild, fast-paced thrusting of their cocks into her body as she swayed back and forth, and then felt the tiny eruption before both men came inside of her together.

She could barely focus as the four men took care of her, cleaned her up, and kissed her everywhere their mouths and lips could reach. Then they wrapped her up in the sheets and Max held her close.

"Rest, love, and when you wake, we'll shower and get something to eat.

She barely could register a coherent thought when Slayer entered her mind.

"Slayer?" she whispered.

"Rest, baby, he's nearby, now rest," Max said and kissed her cheek as he held her back against his front and she drifted off to sleep.

* * * *

Slayer stood by the doorway watching Essie sleep. Max and Ford held her between them. The sight affecting him in too many ways to accept without fear or uncertainty. The reason why, wasn't because he didn't want to commit, or didn't have strong feelings for her, hell, love her. It was because of the monster who haunted her dreams, her life, and threatened to take her from all of them.

He saw Cobra watching over all of them, then glance at him and nodded toward the doorway. His cousin, the leader of the bunch, wanted to talk. Slayer would have to tell him about what he'd learned, about how intense of an individual Blade was, and that somehow, she had gained Blade's full interest and was his obsession.

He stared at Essie's body once more. The tan, toned thighs, her luscious ass, and the possessive hands his cousins had on her. Ford's was over her breast, and Max's was on her thigh with her leg pulled over his thigh. He locked gazes with Cobra. His cousin was tall like him, just about a half an inch shorter, blonde hair cut military short, and muscular, trim, with scars along his body, tattoos of war.

He followed him down the hallway and into the kitchen. It was afternoon, close to four, and they had yet to eat. Their minds, their bodies on one thing—to claim Essie their woman and have her over and over again.

"I see that Max and Ford took out some steaks for dinner," Cobra stated as he looked in the refrigerator and pulled out a water bottle. He glanced at Slayer, offering one. Slayer shook his head and then took the seat closest to the hallway where he could still hear and sort of keep watch.

"You get any sleep?" Cobra asked.

"I'm good."

"That's not what I asked," Cobra replied. Slayer glared at him.

"I don't need a fucking mother."

Cobra raised one of his eyebrows up at him making Slayer feel like a dick for being on edge with Cobra. He trusted Cobra with his life, same with his other cousins. He was just antsy and determined to protect Essie. He knew the only way to do that would be to find this Blade guy and kill the bastard.

"Better lose that attitude before Essie wakes up. Today we need to set down some rules and establish our plan of action. She'll need to go to work, to not feel like a prisoner," Cobra stated.

Slayer leaned on the island and stared at him. "That may not be an option I'm comfortable with."

Cobra exhaled. "What did you find out?"

"I'll make it simple. He's a trained killer. She won't stand a chance against him no matter how much self-defense training or kickboxing she gets. He's hurting people on his quest to find her. Sent several individuals from his apartment, including his landlord into the ICU. The landlord is in critical condition. We don't know who he may or may not have helping him."

"The detectives working the case, have you investigated them?"

"Working on it, but I think Essie's smartest move thus far has been disappearing and not telling the cops where she is. He could have anyone helping him."

Cobra stared at him and then looked away.

"We can't keep her prisoner here. She won't accept that."

"I don't really give a fuck what she thinks she wants. We know Special Forces guys that lose their shit and don't have a sense of reality. We are not going to sugarcoat the potential danger here, Cobra."

"She's our woman, we will do what's necessary to protect her, but she's sensitive, Slayer. You saw her have that panic attack."

"I did see her, and the first thing I thought was if this guy gets close enough to her and she panics, she's as good as dead. She's petite, feminine, sweet, and we've made the joint decision to claim her our woman. We only have one choice here before it gets worse. We need to find this asshole and take him out. I'm more than willing to go hunting while the four of you protect her with your lives."

"No, Slayer. This isn't some mission for the government. It would be murder, plain and simple."

"Do I look like I fucking care?"

"You should care because Essie will not accept this as you defending her and protecting her life. She won't be able to see the military side of this and nor will the cops. Do you think any of us haven't thought of ways we could find this guy and kill him? We're all capable of killing when it's needed, when it's our lives against the enemies, and we're in the war zone or on a mission. This is different."

"How so? Because we're all in the United States of America, a land we're supposed to feel free and protected in? This guy isn't playing by the rules of society, or by the laws of this land. He attacked her, beat her, causing Essie to remain hospitalized for three weeks. On top of that, the slick fuck wired her apartment, watched her with cameras as she showered, dressed and undressed, and slept. The rules of engagement were thrown out the window the moment he attacked her, as far as I'm concerned. You want to do this legit, then give me a plan, some kind of indicator, and we'll make an attempt at a civilized capture. When it fails, when it's our lives, her life, or his, then I don't expect any barriers from you or anyone else. He goes down, Cobra. End of story."

Cobra stared at him and then nodded his head.

"Agreed. We need people we can trust. I can give Vincent Lockatelli a call, and Steel Law knows a lot of people, too," Cobra suggested.

"Why don't you make plans for you and me to meet with Steel and do a conference call with Vincent tomorrow morning when Essie is at work? We'll take it from there."

"Okay, I'll call him now."

Slayer nodded and then looked down the hallway, and he could hear voices and knew they were all probably getting up.

"Hey, she asked for you after we all made love to her. You can't distance yourself because of your fears and concerns. If anything, having her close, making love to her, helps," Cobra told him and then walked out of the room to talk on the phone.

Max and Turbo came out and headed to the refrigerator.

"We'll work on dinner after we take quick showers," Ford said to him and he nodded.

"She's was asking for you, Slayer. She needs you, too," Max told him before he walked out of the kitchen.

Slayer felt so on edge, though. He wanted to tear something apart. To go out and do his thing. Hunt the fucker down and eliminate him. He was feeling like a caged animal and feared being aggressive with Essie. She was so sweet and beautiful. He stood up and made his way to the bedroom. Ford had on his jeans and Essie wasn't there. He panicked

"Where is she?" he asked in a hard tone and Ford scrunched his eyes and then looked Slayer over.

"She's fine, bro. She's going to go take a shower," Ford told him. Slayer looked around the room and then toward the bathroom. He heard the water running.

"She's safe with us, Slayer."

Slayer was quiet and walked deeper into the room. He smelled her perfume, the scent of sex, and a glance toward the bed, all the ruffled sheets and her clothes on the floor reminded him of the night they all shared together. He never imagined it would feel like this. Desperation, loss, emptiness because she wasn't right there in the same fucking room, up against his body where he could hold her and know she was whole and safe and real.

"It's fucking scary man. I know," Ford said, and Slayer locked gazes with his cousin.

"It's like if she's not right here where I can touch her, inhale her shampoo, feel her, it's like I'm empty inside," Ford told him and Slayer was shocked. So, they both felt the same thing.

"You think it's fucking normal?" Slayer asked, and Ford snorted and shook his head.

"I think it's something extra special because I've never felt like this before." Ford looked toward the bathroom door and then back at Slayer.

"We've had sex with other women. Shared other women and none of them, nothing in my life ever felt so fucking powerful and deep as sharing Essie with you and my brothers. She's ours, Slayer. No other men have taken from her body but us. No other men have marked her, come inside of her, and as sick and chauvinistic, hell, barbaric this might sound, I'm fucking relieved. I feel possessive, protective, and desperate. Jesus, the little minx infiltrated where no other ever has." He shook his head and exhaled.

"You got her?" he asked, and Slayer nodded as Ford walked out of the bedroom. His words rang true and mirrored Slayer's feelings. So it wasn't just him. It was all of them. It was that bond, that connection, that special link in a ménage relationship he heard about but thought was bullshit. Essie infiltrated attacked and destroyed that wall he put up over his heart and soul. He just wished his brother, Weiller, and even Kyle were here to experience it all and to love Essie, too.

He felt emotional, and it shocked him. What the fuck?

He pulled off his shirt, undid his pants and discarded the remainder of clothing and made his way into the bathroom. He paused a moment to take in the sight of her in the extra-large walk-in shower. Her back was toward him. Her head hung low as conditioner rinsed from her hair. She had her hands on the wall in front of her. Her full, round ass stuck out, and he could see the series of love bites along her skin. She was theirs. She was his and his cock hardened as he stepped in behind her and gripped her hips.

* * * *

Essie gasped at the feel of large, strong hands gripping her from behind. Then she felt Slayer press up against her back, wrap his arms around her midsection, and suckle her neck.

She exhaled in relief. Here she was staring at the wall, wondering why Slayer hadn't come back into the bedroom to make love to her like the others had. She figured out pretty quickly that he was his own man. That he had some issues of his own with opening up, talking, expressing his emotions and possibly even handling sharing her with his cousins. She didn't understand it all yet. The power and the desire she had for him and his cousins seemed to out weight all rational or potential insecurities she had. She craved them. Wanted them by her side or in the vicinity at all times. She almost felt desperate and was shocked as she stood in the shower alone at home wondering at how alone she felt. How scared and uncertain, and she knew her life had changed.

"How are you feeling? Are you sore at all?" he asked her and kissed her neck, causing her to tilt her head back.

"I feel good, sedated tired," she whispered.

"Hmmm. Too tired to let me make love to you here?" he asked and stroked fingers along her groin and right to her pussy.

She stepped her feet apart, felt his thick hard cock slide between her ass cheeks and she moaned.

He grabbed a fistful of her hair and tilted her head to the side. He kissed her mouth and then pulled back. "I don't think I'll ever get enough of this body, Essie. Of how willing and accepting you are to five lovers like us."

She held his gaze.

"I'm still trying to wrap my brain around it, Slayer."

He thrust his fingers deeper into her cunt.

"Don't get intimidated if my cousins start making some crazy demands, and act possessive. You've...touched us in so many ways," he said and suckled her neck. He rocked his hips against hers and then lowered down, pulled his fingers from her cunt, and replaced them with his cock. She felt the thick, bulbous head against her entrance, then he gripped her hip and tilted her back to accept his entry from behind.

"What about you?" she asked as he started to push his thick, hard cock into her very sensitive cunt.

He slid his hands up her arms and pressed her palms against the shower wall. He gave them a tap. A sure indicator to stay put. She was learning about the men and the control they demanded when they made love to her.

He slid his palms slowly down her hips, pulling them back and then gripping her ass cheeks.

"I'm feeling just as fucking possessive," he stated firmly, then thrust into her balls-deep.

Essie gasped and tightened up, then moaned at the feeling of being filled by Slayer, along with his arousing words.

He kneaded her ass cheeks and stroked his thumb over her anus as he thrust slowly in and out of her pussy.

"You feel incredible, Essie. Every fucking time it gets better and better. I want so much, Essie."

She moaned and thrust back.

"Tell me, Slayer. Oh God, please tell me what you want?" she begged and thrust back against him.

He pressed the tip of his thumb into her ass while he stroked his dick deeper, faster into her cunt.

"I want all of you. I want to mark you my woman in every fucking possible way. I want all other men to know that you belong to me, to my cousins, and if they come near you, God help them because I'll lose my fucking mind," he stated firmly and thrust faster, deeper making her lose her breath. His words, his strokes took her ability to think, to even breathe away from her.

"Slayer," she moaned and then he pulled out, turned her around, grabbed her cheeks, and stared down into her eyes.

"I don't want to fucking come yet. I want to savor every fucking second." He covered her mouth as he kissed her, delving his tongue deeply in exploration, and she held on to him. Ran her palms up and down his body, then gripped his cock. He pulled from her mouth.

"I don't want to come."

She stared at him. "Let me taste you." She lowered down, not waiting for his response, and felt his hand grip her hair and head. She sucked his cock right into her mouth. She swirled her tongue around it, tasted her cream and then slid her fingers into her cunt.

He tugged on her hair,

"Get up here," he demanded in that tone that was all Slayer. The look in his eyes, the expression on his face should have scared her. Maybe it did. Just a little, but in a way that had her pussy clenching for need and her ass, too.

He pressed her up against the wall and stroked fingers into her cunt.

"I want to fuck you everywhere. Claim your mouth, your pussy, and your ass." He kissed her deeply, and he stroked fingers into her cunt then slid his wet digits down and into her ass.

She pulled from his mouth and gasped.

"Do it. Take me. Take whatever you need and want, Slayer. I'm yours."

"What?" he asked and stared down into her eyes. He continued to stroke her ass, and her pussy creamed.

"Take me. Do whatever you need and want. I'm yours," she told him, and was that a smirk?

His fingers pulled out of her ass, and his cock replaced them. He slid into her ass, and she cried out and gripped his shoulders. He pulled slightly back to gain better access and to look at her body.

"You're incredible." He licked his lips and stared at her breasts, cupped them, and stroked the nipples as he thrust into her ass.

She felt so wild and needy. He was such a big man, and she was leaning against the tile wall, thighs spread wide, and her pussy throbbed with need.

He continued to thrust into her ass and play with her breasts, and the sight of his intensity made her crave even more.

She slid her fingers down her chest, her belly and to her cunt. He stopped tugging her nipples and watched as her fingers delved into her cunt.

He stared at her. Their gazes locked.

"Faster, Essie. Finger that cunt the way you like your men to finger you."

She moaned and thrust faster and faster. Her wrists were aching, and she could feel her body begin to tighten. Slayer gripped her hips and thrust faster and faster into her ass.

Her breasts bounced and swayed, her shoulders ached, and she stared at Slayer, who looked wild and out of control. The veins by his eyes stuck out and pulsated.

"Fuck, you're so tight. You're mine, Essie. Every fucking inch of you. We're one, Essie. Say it. You belong to me, and we're one," he demanded.

"You belong to me, and we're one."

"You belong to my cousins and me. Say it," he stated, and she did.

"I belong to you." She took a deep breath and gasped as his cock hammered her ass.

"And your cousins. Yours, Slayer. All yours, every part of me, Slayer. Every part of me." She cried out and came. He roared and shot his seed into her ass. He grunted and moaned and then slowly pulled out of her ass. He adjusted her body against his chest and hugged her tight. He leaned against her and the wall calming his breathing.

They didn't say a word. Neither of them could speak, but Essie wrapped her arms around him best she could and kissed his skin along his shoulders and neck then to his jaw.

He cupped her cheeks, took control as usual and stared down into her eyes.

"Mine. Always," he said, then kissed her.

Chapter Nine

Essie was making photocopies by the copy machine at work. Her mind was on the last several days, and the argument she had with Cobra over her moving in with them. She would love to do that. She felt uneasy, almost insecure without them around her. On top of that, the panic attacks seemed to be getting less aggressive because they were all there to comfort her and calm her down. She was afraid to be instantly dependent on them despite their encouragement and what seemed to be their own desire to have her needy of them at all times. It was confusing, and she was glad she made plans for lunch with Precious.

"So, maybe we can do lunch today?"

Essie jumped and looked to the doorway where Stewart stood watching her. She hadn't known how long he'd stood there and she damned her obsession with the men. They ruled her mind. Their good looks, muscles, and their ability to turn her into a needy sex fiend.

She took a deep breath and smiled.

"I have plans, but thank you anyway," she told him and heard the copier stop. She gathered the papers and tightened up when she felt a hand on her hip and one on her shoulder.

"Essie, I want to take you out. We should talk."

She couldn't believe her train of thought. She imagined any of the men and their reaction to Stewart touching her and asking her to lunch. She needed to be calm here.

She turned around, causing his hand to fall from her shoulder, but his other hand remained on her hip. He stroked it, and she pushed his hand away.

"Don't do that," she said and lowered her eyes and went to walk past him.

"I'm sorry, Essie," he said and stopped her, taking her hand then pulling her back. He repositioned himself in front of her and blocked the doorway. He was a big man. Not exactly appearing as strong or capable like Cobra, his brothers, and Slayer. She swallowed hard.

"What is it?" she asked.

He took a deep breath and released it.

"I get this feeling that you're shy and scared of men. I want you to know that I would never hurt you, Essie. I like you," he said and reached out and stroked her cheek, pushing a strand of hair back. She turned away.

"Listen, Stewart. I think you're a really nice guy, but I'm kind of seeing someone," she told him and he narrowed his eyes and then rubbed his chin.

"Not one of those soldiers from the other night at Carlyle's? Those muscle heads from the dojo?" he asked.

"First of all, they're not muscle heads, they're highly trained soldiers and very nice men."

"Which one?" he asked. She felt that instant uncertainty. She didn't think she was ready to reveal the whole ménage relationship thing with anyone, and never mind with Stewart. She didn't know how the rest of the office would react and the last thing she needed was to be the gossip of the office. As she thought that, she saw one of the women walk by and then look at her and Stewart before smiling and backstepping away. There goes that hope.

Stewart grabbed her arm. "Which one?" he demanded to know.

She tried to yank her arm free.

"Stewart, it isn't any of your business. Now let go of me. I need to finish some things up before lunch."

"You're meeting him? Who is he? The instructor from the dojo or the stray dog?" he seethed.

She narrowed her eyes at him.

"Does it matter which one, because I'm certain if they found out you were touching me, hurting my arm, and saying things like this, they wouldn't be too happy."

"You think I can't take one of them."

"I don't know why you're doing this, Stewart. Move on and ask someone else out. I'm not interested." She yanked her arm free and went to pass him. He pulled her back and kissed her hard on the mouth. He cupped her breast, and she slammed her knee up and then punched him in the nose. He fell back and hit the wall.

Her boss was there.

"What's going on?" he demanded, but she was so angry and upset. She pointed at Stewart.

"You ever, ever try to kiss me again or touch me like that again, and I will sue you for sexual harassment."

"He did what?" her boss, Mo, demanded to know. Others came closer to the room. Including Terry, the secretary.

"This isn't the end of this," Stewart stated in anger.

"It sure as shit is. Grab your stuff, Stewart. You're fired," Mo said, and Stewart glared at Essie and went to step toward her but Mo, all of about five feet seven of the man, stood in front of her.

"Now, or I call the police and let them take you out in handcuffs. You'll be hearing from them either way."

Stewart stormed out of the room, knocking Terry into the wall, and she heard others gasp and then Mo turned her around and faced her, looking at her arm.

"Are you okay? We should call the police and report this."

She thought about some of the rules the men had gone over with her, including in case she got scared, or there was a situation that she needed to call them first, then the police, because they had friends who could keep things on the down low.

"Let me call Cobra Stames."

"Cobra Stames? Why?"

"I can't get into it, but he'll know who we can have come here to file the information on the down low." He narrowed his eyes at her as she whispered that to him.

He had motioned for everyone to go back to their stations and they did.

"You're in some kind of danger?" he asked. She swallowed hard.

"Mo, it has to be done this way."

"I had a feeling something happened to you and that you may have been in hiding. The way you shy away from everyone and even took the back office everyone hates and calls the dungeon."

"Please, Mo."

"Okay, I'll do this your way, but I expect some information."

* * * *

Cobra arrived at Essie's office along with Slayer, Ford, Max, and Turbo. Darius and Steel Law were already there and talking to her in her office. She stood up when she saw them and Cobra noticed her red arm and that she held an ice pack on her knuckles. He pulled her into his arms.

"Are you okay?"

"I'm fine, Cobra, really," she said softly and then others looked her over and asked her questions. She told them about what happened and about Stewart kissing her and touching her and how she punched him in the nose, hurting her hand.

Ford lifted her hand up, removed the ice pack, and narrowed his eyes.

"Where is the asshole now?" he asked.

Her boss Mo was there, and they explained a little about the danger Essie was in and how this situation needed to remain on the down low.

"My God, Essie. I'm so sorry. I can't believe that on top of some crazed stalker looking for you that Stewart went after you today, too.

He's done. However you want to handle this situation is fine with me," Mo told them.

"Good. We may need to hold off on the charges, officially, but Steel and Darius can take the report and file it," Cobra stated.

"We'll take a ride by his place and see if Stewart headed home," Darius said to them.

"We appreciate the help with this. The last thing we need is to publicize what has happened and bring attention to Essie's location," Ford stated.

"Agreed," Steel said.

"We'll head out now," Darius told them and they all shook hands.

"We'll go, too," Cobra said and looked at Slayer.

"Essie can come back to the dojo as we finish things up there for the day," Ford said.

"I was meeting Precious for lunch. Won't I be able to do that still? It's right down the block from the dojo. I could come back to work. I think it will be fine," she said to them.

Cobra stared at her.

"Please, Cobra, it will take my mind off this stupid situation, and I'll be with Precious and right down the block. I doubt Stewart will come looking for more trouble."

"It's two blocks away from the dojo," Slayer stated firmly.

Cobra looked at his brothers and Slayer.

"Turbo and Max will walk you there and when you're almost done, you text them to come meet you to walk you back," Cobra stated firmly.

"Cobra," she started to argue, and he raised one of his eyebrows up at her, and she closed her mouth and nodded.

"Okay, let's do this," Steel said to them.

* * * *

Precious looked at Essie's arm as they sat at the table outside of the café.

"I can't believe that Stewart did that to you. What an asshole. I bet Cobra and Slayer are going to tear into him with Steel and Darius."

"I hope they don't. They were very angry," she said and looked at her knuckles. They were red and swollen.

"Well, I guess they should be proud that you defended yourself and even broke Stewart's nose. Served him right. I guess you'll continue the kickboxing classes, huh?" she teased, and Essie smirked.

"I just reacted. I got so angry. A week ago, I might not have reacted so defensively."

"Ahh, so it has to do with having five lovers, huh?" she asked and took a sip of her ice tea. Essie blushed. She felt her cheeks warmed and then nibbled her bottom lip.

"It's so crazy, and part of why I was looking forward to you and me getting together today."

"Need to talk things through? I know what you mean. I had my own reservations and concerns about my men, and they aren't all Special Forces soldiers like yours are."

Essie stared at Precious. "You're a lot stronger than I am, Precious. You were already trained to defend yourself and take care of yourself. You're amazing. I don't have those same capabilities, and even now, after spending the week with Cobra, Ford, Max, Turbo, and Slayer, I feel weaker."

Precious scrunched her eyes together.

"I don't understand. How could you feel weaker? You just defended yourself against Stewart. Weeks ago, you may have backed down and allowed him to be pushy."

"I suppose you're right. I mean, when he touched me, grabbed my arm, I initially thought about the guys' reaction when they would find out. Then when he forcibly kissed me and cupped my breasts, I lost it. I got angry and reacted."

"That probably has a lot to do with your men."

"You think so, or do you think it's like what Corey says about the moves, the boxing reactions becoming instinctual?"

"I'm sure that had a lot to do with it, but also the fact that you know you have five men backing you up. They're ready to protect you, fight for you, and I assume, inform you of various rules they expect you to abide by."

Essie leaned closer, her eyes widening. "You, too?" she asked.

Precious nodded. "To be honest with you, as independent as I thought I was and wanted to be, my men's rules cause something incredible inside of me, and it's like all I want to do is please them. Crazy, huh?"

"Exactly how I feel. It's like I keep asking myself if I'm becoming clingy, dependent on them for everything both big and small, and is that normal and safe, hell, healthy?"

"Honey, the orgasms are well worth it," Precious said and Essie chuckled, then covered her face with her hands.

She loved having a friend like Precious.

"Hey, I have an idea. How about surprising them with something special of your own, especially after their concerns over today's situation?" Precious suggested.

"What did you have in mind?"

"There's a cute little boutique three blocks from here on Esther Ave. How about we hit it up before you call your men to come get you. Then when they pick you up from there, you can tease them about what may or may not be in the bag."

Essie felt her belly do a series of flip-flops.

"Lingerie, huh? Never shopped for any before."

"Well, you will be now. You have five men to please, and they all have their own fantasies they'll want you to fulfill."

"Let me text Ford and see if they're okay with this."

"Just tell them you'll text them the location of the store shortly."

"They won't go for that. I'll tell them it's a surprise and that I will be three blocks away and with you."

"Good, now let's hope the food comes soon so we'll have enough time to shop," Precious said, and Essie smiled as the waitress headed toward them with their salads and drinks. She couldn't wait to shop in the lingerie store and wondered what each of her men's fantasies with her might be.

* * * *

Cobra, Slayer, Steel, and Law looked around outside of Stewart's small house. No one was answering the door, and his car wasn't in the driveway.

"I guess he didn't head home," Steel said to them.

"Well, all we can do is come back in a little while and see if we can catch him. In the meantime, we'll both swing back later tonight to check things out and speak with him," Darius told them.

Slayer felt uneasy about all of this. It just added to the need to have Essie close to them at all times. He thought about her being out with Precious right now and decided that joining them at the café would be a wise decision.

Cobra's cell phone rang.

"It's Vincent," he said, and they all waited and listened.

"Hey, Vincent. What's going on?" he asked and looked at each of them.

"What?" he asked, and Slayer stared at him. "I'm going to put you on speaker. Slayer, Darius, and Steel are here with me." He put the call on speaker.

"So, what I got so far is that someone with access to the police files has been looking up info on Essie's case. I didn't want to dig further as I caught wind from an inside source that outside detectives took over the investigation and some government guy is involved now. Seems that this Blade guy is wanted for questioning on a murder of a fellow soldier. The guy's body was found in the woods in upstate New York. The local park rangers assumed he died from a self-inflicted gunshot wound. He was a loner. By the time the body was found and transported to the medical examiner's office, it was weeks old. The ME believed that he was murdered and of course it was too late to go back to the crime scene and collect anything," Vincent told them.

"So, how do you know he was murdered and what does this have to do with Blade?" Steel asked.

"This federal investigator, along with two other detectives from the NYPD Special Investigation unit, believe that the guy was killed and Blade is their main suspect. The two men served together, but then something happened in some mission in Iraq. Blade raged about this guy being at fault for getting a few guys killed. Nothing came of it. But from what my sources say, Blade killed him, and they're trying to keep it on the down low."

"Why is that? They know about what he did to Essie and how he's stalking her?" Cobra asked.

"I would assume so, but they are also looking into finding out who has been bringing up Essie's file and trying to find her."

"Shit. Could be Blade has his own person or people helping him," Steel stated.

"Let's assume that's the case. There's nothing in there that states where she is. The best thing Essie did was leave without telling a soul where she was headed," Slayer said.

"But she has family, Slayer. This guy will stop at nothing to get to her," Vincent said.

"He's right, but we already have people watching over her parents and her aunt and uncle. We'll keep watching over Essie. In fact, I think we should get to her now," Slayer added.

"Hey, do you want me to dig deeper to see if I can find out who is looking at her files? Even if the government guy or detectives find out, I can just make something up like the crime mirrors another one I am looking into."

"Yeah, Vincent. Do it and be careful," Cobra said to him.

"Hey, what are all you guys doing together anyway?" Vincent asked.

Cobra explained about Stewart and what happened at Essie's job. He gave him his name and told him how Essie defended herself.

"Son of a bitch. The poor thing must be beside herself. Take care of your woman, and I'll do whatever is necessary on my end. I'll be in touch."

* * * *

"I love these things. I won't be able to choose," Essie said, and Precious chuckled.

She held up a very naughty, sexy red number on a hanger in one hand and then a soft blue sheer teddy in the other hand. "For the naughty and the sweet sides of you, Essie," she teased and chuckled.

Essie laughed. She had a feeling that neither would last long on her anyway. Suddenly she wanted to see her men and be with them.

"I'm going to take both of them. But I don't think they'll be on long."

"Of course not, Essie, but just the look on their faces when you emerge from the bedroom as they anticipate your arrival will be satisfaction enough. To know that with your sexy body, dark blue eyes, and the sexy stare-down you give them makes them all putty in your hands. Oh yeah, so worth every penny," she said, and Essie couldn't help but feel excited. She even grabbed the matching thong panties with the exposed front.

* * * *

"What is taking her so long?" Max asked. He lay on the bed in his boxers waiting for Essie's surprise. She said she wanted to thank them for being there for her and for taking such good care of her.

"I don't know, but for some reason, the anticipation is making my dick fucking hard," Ford stated, and they all agreed.

Slayer stood by the doorway with his arms crossed in front of his chest and Cobra sat in the chair looking serious. They couldn't wait to see her all day, and the fact that Stewart was nowhere to be found, didn't sit right with any of them.

"Essie, come the fuck out," Turbo yelled to her, and Max chuckled.

"That's romantic, Turbo," Max teased him.

"Fuck romantic when my dick is this hard, and I thought of nothing but sinking balls-deep in her all day since the call about fucking Stewart. I don't give a shit," Turbo said and got up and started heading toward the bathroom door when it opened, and he stopped short.

Max sat up. His heart pounded inside of his chest. Essie looked like an angel in blue. The sheer teddy barely reached her midthigh. And her full, large breasts poured from the top showing off deep cleavage and her tan, slim neck. The overlay moved with her hips as she stepped closer into the room. She stared at them all.

"Do you like it? I didn't know if you guys like lingerie or not," she asked them. The color brought out the deep blue in her eyes.

Max heard the low whistles and then mumbled compliments. He walked closer.

"Turn around so I can see it all," he said to her.

She slowly turned around and the overlay lifted with the movement, and she could see that the blue teddy was see through.

He reached out and took her hand. He led her toward the bed.

"You are gorgeous, baby, and I personally love this surprise." When he got to the bed, he sat down and placed his hands on her hips and pulled her between his legs.

"Look at her," he said, and Max rubbed his palms up her hips to her breasts. He cupped them and used his thumbs to stroke her nipples. They immediately hardened and her lips parted.

"This is where you went today and wouldn't tell us?" Turbo asked in that hard tone of his.

"Yes," she said and held his gaze, then moaned because Max stroked her nipples harder. "Max," she moaned.

"You are in for a hell of a night, doll. A hell of a night," he said and then kissed her neck and then the cleavage of her breasts. Ford stepped in behind her and pulled her hands behind her back.

"Oh," she gasped.

"I think what Turbo is getting at, is the spanking that's coming Essie's way for making us worry," Ford stated. He then pulled the sheer overlay down off of her and then raised her arms up above her head and brought them to his shoulders.

"Hold on to me and don't let go," Ford said to her.

The move caused her breasts to push out and her teddy to raise up and reveal some blue silk material.

"What do we have here?" Turbo asked and ran his palm up her thigh as Max continued to stroke her nipples.

"Holy shit," Cobra stated, joining them on the bed. Max saw the sexy blue silk thong panties and the open front. Her very bare, pink pussy was dripping cream.

Ford reached around and stroked a finger into her cunt.

"Oh God," she said and began to lower her arms.

"Don't you dare move. You stay with your hands up above your head and against Ford's shoulders. Step those legs apart and allow us full access to what is ours," Slayer ordered, and she closed her eyes and moaned louder. Max could hear how wet she was as Ford thrust fingers into her cunt.

Max lifted the teddy up to her neck and then leaned forward to suckle a breast. She was rocking her hips.

"I need her," Max said and pushed down his shorts and lowered back to the bed.

Ford pulled fingers from her cunt.

"We all do," he said and then lifted her up to straddle Max's waist. They pulled off the teddy.

"Ride him," Ford ordered, and she lifted up and sank down on his cock still wearing the panties with the open front.

"Oh God. Oh," she moaned.

"Her punishment, Ford," Cobra stated firmly.

Smack.

Smack.

Smack.

Smack

"Oh!" she cried out and came after the fourth smack to her ass cheeks by Ford.

"Fuck. I need it hard. Move," Max yelled out, and Ford stepped back. Max rolled her to her back. Lifted up, stood, and dragged off the panties, spread her thighs, and licked her from anus to pussy back and forth.

"Max. Oh my lord," she moaned and reached for his head as he ate at her cunt.

She thrust and lifted her pelvis up and down.

Max growled feeling desperate to claim her, and he knew his brothers needed her, too.

He aligned his cock with her cunt and thrust into her hard and fast.

She gripped his shoulders, hugged his hips with her thighs as he fucked her.

She gripped him and moaned.

"More. I need more," she stated, and he rolled over so she straddled him. He hung his legs over the bed and then Ford joined in. Smack.

Smack.

"Ford," she reprimanded.

"Open those thighs and get that ass ready for cock," Cobra told her. He grabbed her hair and face and kissed her on the mouth. Max felt her jerk and then grunt into Cobra's mouth as Ford. Pressed lube to her ass then slid into her ass balls-deep. Max and Ford thrust into her in sync. Max never felt so wild and needy in his life.

Ford exploded a few strokes later then pulled out.

Cobra released her lips and then ran his hands over her ass as Max thrust up into her.

"I feel so tight. Oh God, I need more," she demanded, and Max came next.

She was immediately lifted up and placed on all fours. Max and Ford moved out of the way, and Cobra, Slayer, and Turbo moved closer.

"Allow us full access to you. Relax those muscles. This body, every fucking inch of you belongs to us, Essie. Understand me?" Cobra demanded.

"Yes. Oh God, yes, Cobra."

She panted for breath.

* * * *

Cobra was desperate. All this craziness around them and the danger surrounding their woman was taking its toll on each of them. He was the leader, their commander and he felt responsible for resolving the situation and bringing Essie safety and security forever. She completed their family, their team.

He massaged her back, her ass, and thighs, and then back up to her shoulders. He pressed her chest to the bed and lifted her hips and ass up into the air.

He massaged the globes as Slayer took the overlay from the teddy and tied her wrists with it. He attached it to the bed frame, and she moaned and thrust downward.

"Someone likes to be restrained," Slayer said and then stroked his cock. He brought it toward Essie's cheek, and she turned sideways trying to get at it.

"Oh no you don't. When I come and mark you, it will be in your sweet, wet cunt. Now spread those thighs. Cobra has something for you," Slayer said to her.

She did as he said and Cobra aligned his cock with her cunt from behind and slid right into her pink soft flesh.

He closed his eyes and then refocused on her as he thrust and stroked into her cunt. The sight of her naked body, her toned shoulders, round full ass, and tight, puckered hole called deeply to him. He gripped her hips and then stroked faster, deeper.

"Come all over my cock baby. Come all over," he demanded and then Turbo slid his hands along her ass and pushed lube into her hole.

"Fuck that is hot. Look at her asshole suck my fingers inside. She needs cock there next." Turbo said and then ran his palm up her spine to the back of her head. He leaned closer and kissed her shoulder then whispered into her ear.

"Want my cock in your ass, baby?"

"Yes. Yes, yes, yes," she said.

"Fuck," Cobra grunted and came.

He slid out and gave her ass a smack.

"Oh."

"You little vixen. You're in for it tonight. We're just getting started," Cobra said and winked at Slayer.

* * * *

Turbo licked his lips and stared at her back, and her ass lifted high and glistening with lube.

He got in behind her and ran his palms up her legs from ankles to thighs.

"So, you thought you'd surprise us with lingerie? I think we all agree that we like it. We also like you being submissive and accepting our control and command. Tell me, Essie. How aroused are you right now, with your wrists tied and restrained, open to our ministrations?"

he asked and lowered down and licked down her spine to her ass crack then nipped her ass cheek.

"Very aroused, Turbo. Please, stop teasing me."

"Oh, but it was okay for you to make us wait and then tease us with that sexy teddy and panties?"

"That was the point," she said to him, and Max chuckled.

"She needs discipline, Turbo," Slayer said to him.

"That she does," Turbo said and then fisted his cock and teased her entrance. He stroked the thick, hard muscle back and forth from pussy to anus. He slid the tip up into her cunt and then pulled it out as she moaned. She started to wiggle and then grunt.

"Turbo," she said his name and sounded angry. He leaned over her and continued to torture her privates.

"Yes, baby, what do you need?"

"You."

"My what?" he asked and nipped her ear lobe.

"Your, your…cock," she said.

"Where do you need it?" She didn't answer but moaned.

He slid the tip of his cock back into her pussy.

"Here?" she moaned.

He pulled it out.

"Or here?" he asked and nudged the tight opening to her asshole.

"Anywhere," she commanded.

"Oh no. You need to specify where you want his cock, Essie. No being shy. You're our woman, and we need to hear you tell us where you want our cocks. Tell him where, Essie," Slayer commanded as he slid his palm along her back and then gave her ass a hard slap.

"My ass, damn you," she yelled out, and the others chuckled.

"Fuck that ass, bro," Ford chimed in.

"With pleasure," Turbo said and slowly began to push his cock into her tight ass. She wiggled, and he gripped her hips and then shoved all the way in. He closed his eyes and exhaled. Felt Essie exhale, too. The sight and sounds drove him insane.

He looked at her body and at his cock lost in her ass. Slayer was caressing her hair with one hand and stroking his cock with his other hand.

She was restrained and naked, her entire backside exposed to him and it drove him insane. He thrust his hips and focused on feeling her, possessing her the way he needed. He ran his palms up and down her shoulders and back, then to her hips.

He pressed fingers to her cunt but didn't push all the way in as he teased her. He felt her pussy spasm. They each made her come. She was so responsive to them. She was their woman now and forever.

"Mine. Fucking mine," he commanded and thrust and thrust until he started to feel weak in the knees as he came. He roared loudly and then lowered over her as he eased out of her ass and he kissed her tenderly. He eased out and off of her, and Slayer took over as Essie moaned.

* * * *

Slayer rolled her to her back, adjusted the restraints and looked at her.

"You are a fucking angel," he said and then knelt between her legs and held himself above her as he absorbed the sight.

Her lips were wet and parted, her dark blue eyes glossy with desire. Her chest all blotchy, her cheeks flushed, and her chest heaved up and down.

He ran his palm from her throat to her breast, played with the nipple, and then played with her belly ring. He stroked a finger over her clit, and she tightened up and moaned.

"Sore?" he asked, and she immediately shook her head.

"You probably wouldn't tell me if you were. You like our cocks, don't you?"

"Yes," she said and then licked her lips. He felt about ready to explode. Watching his cousins make love to her like this was inspirational. It seemed to get better and better and even more intense.

He slid his palm along her belly and up her breast, cupping the large mound, then tugging the nipple.

"Such the perfect body. Made for us."

He lowered down and kissed her on the mouth. She went to move her hands, and they fell back to the comforter.

"I want to touch you."

"I want to possess you, control you, own you in every way," he admitted and then gripped her hips and spread her thighs with his thighs. His cock tapped at her entrance.

"You do already."

"I need more."

"Then take me how you want. I'm yours," she told him.

He lifted up and began to slide into her tight, wet channel.

"That you are," he said then rammed balls-deep into her cunt.

He closed his eyes, and she came. Just like that, she orgasmed, lubricating his strokes and adding to the excitement of making love to her. He thrust into her over and over again and then reached up and undid the ties. She immediately cupped his cheeks.

"I'm ruined forever. I'll never want any other men than the five of you. Please don't ever leave me, Slayer. Don't ever give up on me, on us," she said to him and his heart ached.

"Never," he said and plunged his tongue into her mouth and ravished her as he made love to her. He rocked and thrust, and she countered. He was so emotional, so connected to her that when she cried out her release, he followed and came inside of her and images of her pregnant with their baby entered his mind. He wanted things with her he never thought he ever wanted.

"Forever, Essie. Forever, I love you," he said.

"I love you, too, Slayer. I love all of you," she stated and kissed his neck as he held her close, then rolled to the side to not crush her but keep her safe and secure in his arms where she belonged and where he needed her to be.

Chapter Ten

"Essie! Essie, damn it, focus!" Slayer yelled at her as Ford had her pinned on the mat in the dojo with her arms above her head. She was starting to go into a panic attack.

"Slayer, calm down. She's trying," Cobra said to her.

"She isn't trying hard enough." He raised his voice as Ford released her arms. Tears were in her eyes and she tried submerging them, but she was scared. She didn't want to be weak or look weak in front of Slayer or the others. They were soldiers. Men who didn't really show emotion never mind backing down from anything. Not even things that challenged their capabilities. She wanted to make them proud, happy, encouraged by her ability to beat the panic attacks, and now learn combative self-defense moves that soldiers learned. She kept thinking about that night Blade attacked her and how badly she was injured. She knew this time he would kill her if he got his hands on her. All she wanted to do was cuddle up in one of her men's arms and hide from the possibility.

"Ease up, Slayer. I know that it's important she learns as precaution, but you have to remember that she was attacked before, and nearly beaten to death. All these scenarios bring back memories of that. Throw in her panic attacks, and she's fighting against a lot of barriers besides her attacker," Magnum added. Precious was there, too, for moral support. She looked at her.

"Teach her where to strike initially to incapacitate her attacker," Cobra suggested.

"You mean like kill zones? Hand-to-hand combat?" Ford asked as Slayer stood in the corner looking angry with his arms crossed and staring at them.

Essie sat up.

"Are there certain spots of the body I could aim for to buy me time to run?" she asked, forcing herself to think like a survivor and not a victim. One glance at Precious, and her wink and then nod, and she knew she asked the right question and was showing these men she wasn't a pushover.

"There are numerous places to strike. She's short though and would be exposing her body to some hits in the process," Magnum said and approached.

"Let's try a few things," he said and then approached Essie. He told her where to strike as he made a move. She was determined to give this a try. As Magnum wrapped her around the waist and hoisted her up in the air, Ford told her what to do and how to slam her palms hard against Magnum's ears. He wore protective head gear so after the first few times he told her to hit as hard as she could, that the gear would protect him. She did.

"Good. Just like that, and when I falter…" he said, and Ford picked up, continuing to give instruction. She was feeling a little more empowered, but pretty tired as they ended the session and talked about the next class. She looked over toward where Slayer had been standing, and he wasn't there. She looked at the doorway and at the window and no sign of him.

"You did well, baby. It's only the beginning of your training. It will come easier, and you'll learn," Cobra said. She nodded, and he pulled her into his arms and hugged her. She hugged him back feeling the most secure, most content in her lovers' arms. She went into the lady's locker room and took a quick shower, dried her hair, and then dressed for work. When she came into the empty hallway, she saw Slayer standing there. He looked her over.

"You ready?" he asked. He was going to drop her off at work and then Cobra and he or one of the others would pick her up after work.

"Not yet," she said, and he stopped walking, turned around, and stared down at her. She wore high heels, a skirt that hit her thighs midway, and a sleeveless white blouse. He eyed her over and narrowed his eyes at her as she stepped closer to him. She dropped her bag and then took his hands. He tightened up, but she pushed on despite how intimidated Slayer was and looked. She pulled his arms around her waist and placed his hands on her ass. She then slid her palms up his chest and held his gaze.

"I love you, Slayer. I love your cousins, too, and just so you know, I don't want to learn these self-defense things. I don't want to think about ever becoming a victim again. What I focus on, and what I want, is to stay safe in your arms, in your cousins' arms, in your beds, right beside you where I know no one, nothing, can ever hurt me."

He stared at her. She felt his palm slid along her ass and squeeze her snugger to him.

"I want that, too, and I love you, too. So much that it angers me you need to learn these things and be in a room and fight to defend yourself. That's my job now and my cousins' jobs."

"I know, but it's better to be prepared, sort of, instead of oblivious and unwilling to face the realities of life. It isn't a bad thing."

"How so? You're sweet and beautiful and rolling around on the mats grappling. I don't like it."

"I think all of this. You guys making love to me, claiming me your woman and protecting me, as well as the classes here at the dojo and the training, have helped with lessening the panic attacks and building up my self-confidence. I was sort of a scaredy cat before I met all of you."

"Sort of?" he teased and stroked her cheek. She blushed.

"You've taught me a lot, and each of you is so special to me. You're my first and only lovers ever."

"That we are, little virgin. No other men but my cousins and I, got it?"

"Oh yeah. Well, actually…I may need some convincing after work tonight."

"Oh really?" he asked and gave her ass a smack. She hugged him tight and kissed his neck.

"What's going on in here?" Ford asked opening the door.

"Make-out session. Come here," she said to him. Ford whistled out to the lobby, and he closed the door and pulled her into his arms and kissed her tenderly. She felt the second set of hands on her hips from behind and then heard Turbo's voice.

"I have the keys to the storage room," he teased and suckled her neck and began to unzip her skirt. She pulled from Ford's mouth.

"Turbo," she reprimanded.

"We got the door first. Go," Cobra ordered, and Turbo lifted her up over his shoulder and ran her down the corridor to what must be the storage room. Ford and Max followed.

"Lift that skirt, baby. We're going to fill you up before work," Turbo said and pulled off his shirt and started to unbutton his pants. She didn't know how to respond, but then one look at Ford whipping his cock out and licking his lips, and she was game. "I love you guys, but you're crazy."

"Crazy about you," he said and then pushed down her skirt and panties, lifted her up, and pressed her against the wall filling her pussy with cock. She exhaled and then moaned.

"So, I'm not the only one who gets aroused grappling with my men," she said and gasped and Ford pumped harder and faster.

"Fuck no, baby, you sure as shit aren't. In fact, I think we're going to be using the mats at the house for a lot more than self-defense training," Max stated.

"Oh yeah, I'm in," Turbo said, and Essie chuckled, loving her men with all her heart and knowing that life didn't get any better than this.

* * * *

"Don't kill me. I said I'll do it. I'll fucking do it," Stewart said and rubbed his hands on his pants. *This fucking guy dressed in camouflage pants and shirt showed up out of nowhere asking about him and Essie.* Stewart knew instantly that this was the guy who hurt Essie. The one his cousins told him about. This was Stewart's chance to save Essie, and to make her boyfriends look like assholes. If he did what this guy said and brought him to the office, then he could fight the guy, get the knife away, and save her life. Then she would want Stewart. It looked like his plan had come together on its own.

"You alert anyone to my presence, and you're dead. I'll slit your fucking throat," he said.

"I won't. I'll cooperate," Stewart said.

"Where's the office and where is the key? I need to know who is in there with her."

"It's on Beach Road and an insurance agency. The back entrance is on Clover Street. I have the key on my keychain, and it leads to the back door and then her office is right there. She hides there, afraid to be out in the main offices."

The guy narrowed his dark black eyes at him.

"Why?"

"Because she's scared all the time and shy. Not around me, though. She talks to me."

The guy cocked his head and looked him over. He brought the knife up to Stewart's throat. "You fuck her?"

"No. No, man, no. We're friends," he stated.

"Where's the fucking key?" he asked.

Stewart reached for the keys. "This one."

"She'll never be yours, Stewart. Never."

Stewart gasped as the knife stuck into his side. The crazy bastard stabbed him. "No...but I helped you."

"You want what's mine, and anyone who tries to take her dies, too." He grabbed Stewart as Stewart tried to move and he gripped his head and neck and snapped it.

* * * *

Essie was typing away on the computer in her office. Every so often, she would sigh and then chuckle at what happened at the dojo. Her men made love to her, well, fucked her actually, in the storage supply closet. Jesus, it was wild and so were they. So much such that she wound up completely naked, her ass spanked and fucked, and so sedated it took an additional shower and an espresso to get her to walk into work and face the full day ahead of her.

Jesus, she had it bad for them.

She thought she heard the back door open and close and figured that her boss was going out for a cigarette. So when the floor creaked, and she turned around, the last person she expected to see was Blade.

She shoved away from the desk and stood up. He stared at her.

"Essie," he whispered as if he almost didn't believe it was her. There was something in his eyes. Some lost expression that made her respond calmly.

"Blade, what are you doing in South Carolina?" she asked, her voice cracked. She tried to ease back toward the table and the cell phone. Could she call 911?

He stepped closer. Eyed her over and she saw the knife on his hip. She started to shake the closer he got to her.

"Essie, I need a copy of the McGuire contract," Mo stated, coming into the room. Immediately, Blade grabbed him and shoved him up against the wall. She reached for the phone as she screamed. She hit the autodial for Cobra and then dropped the phone on the desk to grab Blade's arm.

"Blade, don't. Please, Blade," she begged of him.

Mo started to slide down the wall, his eyes wide and scared. Blade had him by the throat.

"No, Blade, please. I'll do whatever you want. Don't hurt my boss. He's a nice man. Let him go, please," she begged as she held on to the arm that held Mo by the throat. He looked at her.

"You'll leave with me now?"

"Yes. Yes, just don't hurt him or anyone else. Please," she pleaded.

He released Mo and Mo fell to the rug coughing. She bent down and caressed his hair. "I'm sorry, Mo." She screamed out as Blade grabbed her and pulled her up. "Come now," he demanded.

"No. Don't take her. Don't." Blade pulled out his knife. She screamed. "Don't, Blade." She put herself in front of Mo. Blade was breathing through his nostrils hard, and they flared out, and his eyes looked crazed and red-rimmed.

"Please, Blade. Let's go. Just you and I and we can talk," she said to him. She was shaking so hard. Blade pulled her along with him and out the back door.

There was a truck there, and he got her into it and then gripped her hair. "Don't try to escape, Essie. Don't do it. I won't be able to handle it, Essie. I'm already on edge," he said to her. She saw the blood on his shirt. Had he killed someone already? Had he hurt one of her men? She felt the tears spill from her eyes, then heard screaming by the back door. Mo had her cell phone, and Terry was crying. Blade stepped on the gas and then held her hand with one firm hand and didn't let go. He sped through town, and she prayed that her men would find her before he took somewhere and finished what he started months ago.

* * * *

"We need to get to Essie. Call Slayer now. He's in town. Blade is in town," Steel said to Darius as they discovered Stewart dead in his house.

"Slayer, Blade is in town. You need to get to Essie and let her know now," Darius told him over the phone.

"What the fuck do you mean in town? How the hell do you know?"

"He killed Stewart. He stabbed him and broke his neck."

"Wait, hold on a minute. We're getting a call from Essie now," Slayer told him, and he listened.

"Jesus, he's there. She somehow dialed Cobra's number. We're in the trucks and heading that way."

"We'll meet you." As Steel and Darius got into their cruisers, they heard the 911 radio call go off and about Essie being abducted and Mo getting hurt. They got the description of the vehicle and Darius called Ford and gave him the license plate description and direction the truck was headed.

"Get to her, guys, before that fucking psycho kills her," Darius said aloud as Steel sped toward the highway and the last place they spotted the truck heading.

* * * *

"We have to get to her fast, or he'll kill her. He'll slit her fucking throat or break her neck like he did to Stewart," Cobra stated.

"He can't get that far. The police are already responding. State police will block the roadways. The only way for him to head was the side roads," Ford stated. Just then Darius called again.

"Lake Side Road near the campsite. He's headed there. You guys should be the closest," Darius told them.

"It's up around the bend. We'll get there in time. We have to," Max yelled. Cobra sped up and took the turn super fast. They saw nothing but three different roads leading up to separate campsites.

Cobra stopped the truck. "Which fucking way do we go? Which one? If we choose wrong, then what?" he yelled and banged the steering wheel. The sound of tires squealing came up behind them. Darius and Steel in one car and several state police cars.

"We don't know which road," he yelled out the window.

"We split up. Don't worry, we'll find her," Darius said and then gunned up the road to the left. The other trooper cars went to the right and Cobra and the others headed up the middle road.

"I got a bad fucking feeling," Turbo said and got his weapon ready.

"Just be fucking ready to take a shot if need be. We have to be careful," Slayer said and then Cobra slowed the truck down the further up the road they headed. They were passing small cabins and cottages. They looked for any signs of the vehicle or tire marks, anything. Darius radioed in.

"The roads meet up at the top. One of the troopers comes up here often for fishing. No matter what, we'll meet up."

"Okay, keep a look out for the truck. There are lots of hidden drives and homes."

Cobra told him.

"Got it."

* * * *

"Let go of me. It's over. The police are coming for you, Blade, just give it up," she said to him as he dragged her from the truck and along the path to a cabin. He had a shotgun, ammo, and led her through the trees and a small path, then to a cabin. It was way back from the road. She was so scared, but if the police, if her men didn't come quickly, they may not find her, or by the time they figured out which cabin she could be dead. She needed to think, to help them find her.

She felt her ankle slightly twist and she nearly lost her high heel. The thought hit her hard as she let the heel fall off and pretended to still walk with both, then discarded the other the closer they got to the cabin. Hopefully, they would find her heels.

He got to the door and opened it, then shoved her inside.

"Sit down. There." He pointed to a chair in the center of the room. She didn't move, and he was in her face, gripping her shoulders hard. The man was as big and tall as Slayer. Had a more intense, dangerous look in his eyes, and she felt like he wasn't human.

"Why are you doing this, Blade? What is it that you want?" she asked him and he pushed her into the chair. He pointed at her.

"You," he said firmly.

"Don't move," he stated. She watched him undo the duffel bag and place different guns on the floor and by the window. He was going to hold her hostage and take out anyone who approached the cabin. He would kill her men, the police, anyone who tried to help her.

She didn't know what to say or do. She watched him as he paced then took a deep breath and released it. He turned and looked at her. This was the man who attacked her one night and put her in the hospital for weeks. The man who placed cameras around her apartment without her knowing and watched her. She shivered as he walked closer and looked at her body. He was the man who broke into her car, her apartment and promised to find her.

He stood right next to her and when he reached out, she clenched her eyes closed and waited to feel the strike. It didn't come. Instead, he stroked her skin.

"So soft, beautiful," he whispered, and she blinked her eyes open and stared up at him. Blade had dark black eyes, long, dark black hair that looked greasy like he hadn't showered or gotten a haircut in a long time. His eyes were rimmed red, and his hands shook slightly.

He continued to caress her cheek and then slid his palm down her arm, his knuckles grazed her breast, and she shuddered and pulled to the side and away from him.

He paused, narrowed his eyes at her and squinted.

"Where to begin," he said and then lowered down as if he would kiss her.

"Get away from me," she stated. He paused and eased back.

"I know I screwed up the first time. I'm making that all up to you."

"You mean trying to kill me? Leaving me for dead? Hospitalized for weeks?" she rambled.

"I wasn't right then. I let my mind win over what was really happening. Not this time," he said and gripped her chin, lowered his mouth to hers, and kissed her. She pushed against his chest, and he straddled her on the seat. He squeezed his thighs against her where she couldn't move, and she tried striking his body, but he was made of steel. The fear, the terror that she didn't stand a chance, came crashing over her body.

He released her lips and then grabbed her hands, pulling them behind her back. He held them with one hand as she cried out in pain, her shoulders feeling like they'd snapped. He used his other hand to undo the top two buttons on her top. Tears spilled from her eyes. "Don't do it. Don't touch me." She begged that he wouldn't rape her.

"I want to see what belongs to me. What I was forced to watch from a distance as you slept, as you showered, and dressed and undressed," he told her, staring at her lips as he undid the next three buttons. Her full breasts emerged in the lace bra, and she felt the tears continue to roll down her over her breasts.

"Don't cry, Essie. We're meant for one another. I'm going to protect you from all the men who want to hurt you."

He lowered his mouth to her cleavage where the tears had fallen, and he licked her there. She shuddered. He continued to suckle her skin, move along her throat, and then to her lips.

"Stop. I don't want this," she said to him. He gripped her wrists tighter and lifted up.

Cupping her cheek with his free hand, he stroked her jaw with his thumb.

She stared at him and felt he was lost in thought. She wouldn't stand a power war with this monster, so she had to think out of the box.

"Why did you choose me that night at the club?" she asked him. He blinked his eyes and then released her chin.

"You're special, Essie. Not some whore, or tramp looking for a good time. You didn't belong there, not alone and not with those girls you called friends. I bet you didn't know that they were jealous of you." She swallowed hard. He smirked and nodded, then continued to touch her skin. He ran a palm along her arm and to her breast.

"They approached me and told me they would accept a date. Said you were a prude," he told her and then lowered down, licked his lips, and slid his tongue into the cup of her bra. She pulled from his hold and shoved at him hard. She stood up, and he reached for her. She reacted and slapped him across the face. He countered with a strike to her jaw, sending her onto her back on the floor.

He reached for her, pulled her up and against him, then slammed her back against the wall with her straddling his hips. She cried out, and he gripped her head and slammed it back against the wall, stunning her. Her vision blurred, and she slapped and clawed at his face and chest. Then they heard the creak of the floorboard outside, and he dropped her to the floor, ran for the shotgun, and fired through the wood. She heard the roar of pain. She didn't know who it was.

Cobra? Slayer? Ford? Max? Turbo? Oh God. She lay on the floor, head aching, lips bleeding, and jaw aching badly. He was going to kill anyone who came close. She couldn't let her men die. Let innocent people die trying to save her. She could hear the commotion. They were pulling away whoever was shot.

"Give yourself up. It's over," she said and tried sitting up. The pain in her head and her back was excruciating. She could feel the bruises form on her shoulders and spine. Blade had shoved her so hard against the wall.

She looked at him. He seemed crazed, wild, and she was beginning to think this cabin would be her grave.

"They're not going to get to you, Essie. You're mine, and I'm here to protect you."

"They're not the enemy," she screamed at him.

"They are the enemy. You don't know. They're always out there waiting to attack. Waiting to take us out. I know. I've seen past their disguises, Essie," he told her and he was so serious, so intense in his statement she knew he wasn't mentally stable, but actually thought they were at war.

"I think you need help."

He glared at her and then adjusted his weapon and moved toward the window.

"Anyone who comes close to this cabin will die."

* * * *

"Thank God she left those heels or we would be searching up the wrong path," Cobra said to Slayer. They were approaching the cabin when they saw the other troopers closing in and then suddenly shots were fired. They all ducked. The one trooper went down, and two others grabbed him and pulled him out of the line of fire.

"What the fuck are they doing?" Steel asked and hurried forward.

"She is probably so scared right now," Max said to them.

"We're here, and we'll put together a plan. She's smart," Cobra said.

"Here. I gathered what we had access to," Ford said, and he and Turbo handed out the weapons and then gear. The troopers gave them bulletproof vests, and as they got ready to make a move, Darius told them that federal agents and the detectives from New York were coming up the pathway.

"Like I give a fuck? They already lost their chance to help Essie. She's in this situation because of them," Cobra stated.

As they approached the introductions began.

"We're not allowing you to take lead on this. He's Special Forces, and we know how to think like him and get in there," Slayer said to the agent and the detectives.

"Is that so? Because last I checked he wasn't dealing with a full deck. He killed a detective he had gather information for him who was also an undercover agent," the federal agent told him.

"We don't have time for this shit. The longer he has her inside of there the worse it will be," Cobra told them.

"It's our investigation, our case. You're soldiers, not agents. Our team goes in first," the agent said, and they started arguing with them.

"You're going to get your men killed. He just took pot shots at the state police and one guy is down. Let these men handle it like a military operation. It's their woman Blade has in there. Let them do this," Darius said to them.

"We get the arrest," the agent said, sounding like he was worried about the exposure to the agency and not saving lives.

"No promises. You might get a body, but you're more than welcome to put handcuffs on it and pretend," Slayer said and walked away. Cobra followed along with Max, Turbo, Ford, Darius, and Steel.

* * * *

"Don't be scared, angel. I'll protect you with my life," he said to her, holding her in his arms on his lap. He sat on the chair and had put the back against the wall. His long gun leaned against the corner next to him, and a huge hunting knife lay on his thigh in a holder. She was shaking, trying to come up with a plan. Would she have enough time to run if she grabbed the knife, stabbed him, and ran for the door?

He stroked her hair and kissed her neck. Her back was against his front. She was shivering with fear and disgust as he inhaled against her neck then stroked her breasts. He ran his palms down her thighs and up under her skirt. She had to trick him. Get him to think she liked him touching her and then she would take the knife and use it. No one was coming in. She shifted, and he gripped her breast hard.

"Oh. Please don't hurt me. I was just going to turn around and face you," she said to him and lay still, waiting for his acceptance.

He released her breast and guided her as she turned. He opened his thighs wider, so she was forced between them. She stood, and he eased up and cupped her ass cheeks while he held her gaze.

"Hands on my shoulders," he ordered. She slowly complied, and when she touched his shoulders and felt the steel, she shivered with fear. She thought about her men. They were out there and if when they tried to break in to rescue her Blade would kill them just like he shot and probably killed the other man who tried to get in. She closed her eyes and willed the dizziness and the pain away. She had to be strong. She couldn't be weak and fragile.

She ran her hands up over his shoulders as he caressed her ass and then up her hips. He squeezed her so tight she gasped.

"We should have made love that night. It went all wrong," he told her.

Tears rolled down her cheeks. She couldn't help it. She was petrified. She'd really begun to shake, and he noticed it.

"I scare you still?" he asked her. She nodded.

"I'll make it up to you," he said and pulled her closer to kiss her and plunge his tongue in deeply. She let him access her mouth, and she slid her hand down his shoulders and to his arm then lower to his thigh. He gripped her tighter, and she felt his other hand press between her legs under her skirt and just as his fingers grazed her panties, she made her move.

Essie gripped the knife, pulled up, and then slammed it into his side. She pulled it out as he roared in anger and shove her hard to her throat. She dropped the knife, grabbed her throat, and looked at him hunched over, reaching for the blade.

Run, Essie, run.

She damned herself for hesitating and hurried to the door, pulled it open, and heard him roar. She felt the slice to her side and then she tumbled down the steps, hitting her forehead. She heard yelling and guns firing loudly.

Then hands were on her, slowly rolling her over. "Essie. Oh God, Essie."

Slayer.

"Fuck, she's been stabbed, and she hit her fucking head so hard when she fell forward. Jesus," Cobra yelled, and she blinked the tears from her eyes as a shirt was pressed to her head.

"I've got one for her arm," Max said.

"Here, Slayer, use this on her side," Turbo stated.

An ambulance is coming up now," Ford said. She looked at them.

"I fought him. I was brave, not weak," she whispered and coughed.

Someone touched her throat.

"She's bruising up here," Ford said.

"Where's the fucking ambulance?" someone yelled out.

"You sure are brave. Fucking crazy. We were making our way inside," Max said to her.

"He said he would kill you all." She whispered, voice cracking.

She heard the sirens and then saw the anger and fear on her men's faces as they were forced to step back as paramedics arrived.

"Don't leave me again," she said to them.

"Never again, Essie. We're here, baby. Always," Cobra said to her.

She closed her eyes and willed her body to relax. Blade was dead. Her men were safe and alive. It was finally over.

Epilogue

Essie fixed her hair in the mirror and let the red lace, silk nighty fall into place. The top fell just barely covering her nipples. She wore no panties and no overlay. She was bringing out the big guns because her men had yet to make love to her because of the concussion and her stitches. Those stitches on her arm and side were taken out a week ago, and she was feeling ready for action.

She slowly opened the bathroom door to the bedroom and saw them gathered around reading, looking at the laptop, watching TV, and fully clothed.

She cleared her throat but didn't show her attire.

They all looked up.

"I need something. So very badly I ache," she said and made a pouty face. They all stopped what they were doing. Slayer scrunched his face and immediately headed toward her.

"No. Stay right there. I have to handle this myself because I can't count on any of you."

"What, baby?" Cobra asked.

"What do you mean you can't count on us? If something hurts or you need something we're here for you," Max said.

"We've been telling you that for over a month," Ford said.

"What's this all about? Tell us, and we'll help," Turbo stated firmly.

She shook her head.

"I found my own help because you guys are slacking," she said and then hit the button and pushed open the door revealing a thick, long vibrator in pink, and her sexy negligee. The expressions on their faces were priceless. She had to be sure to thank Precious for picking this up for her the other day and dropping it off. What a great idea.

"Essie," Slayer stated through clenched teeth.

"You won't give me what I need, so I had to improvise." She started to lift her teddy and bring the vibrating dildo underneath when Turbo stomped across the bedroom, lifted her up, and brought her to the bed.

She gasped and then chuckled as he removed her nighty and they all started to undress.

She locked gazes with Turbo who now held the vibrator in his hand. Someone pulled her arms above her head and a quick glance up and she saw it was Max.

"That's pretty impressive, Essie, but nothing like the real deal," Cobra stated, standing there stroking his cock.

"I forget," she teased, and it was on. Turbo lowered down and licked her cunt, got it all wet and made her pussy cream and then he slowly began to push the vibrator into her channel.

"Turbo," she reprimanded.

"I thought you were looking for additional cock to fill you up?" he asked and the others chuckled.

"Just your cocks. The real deal," she said, and he smiled, pulled out the vibrator and then aligned his cock with her cunt and filled her up. She moaned and exhaled.

"Finally," she said.

"Oh, she is in for a hell of a night," Cobra said.

"I get to spank her ass first," Slayer told them.

"I get to fuck her ass first," Max said.

"I get her mouth," Ford stated.

"I am going to make her beg for mercy," Turbo promised and began to thrust so fast and deep she couldn't help but to moan and wonder if maybe the vibrator had pushed them too far.

Then again, their expressions on their faces were priceless, and her behavior was their fault anyway. They built up her confidence.

Showed her what true love really was like, and made her fall in love with them. She was a changed woman. A woman in love with five sexy Special Forces soldiers, and there was no challenge she wouldn't accept.

Turbo pulled out of her cunt and flipped her onto her belly, then lifted her up as Max slid underneath her. She gripped his shoulders and immediately sank her pussy over his cock. She closed her eyes and moaned.

"We created a monster," he said.

Smack. Smack. Smack.

"Oh," she exclaimed. Turbo pressed lube to her ass after he spanked her.

He whispered into her ear, "How long have you had the vibrator and have you used it before?" She gulped.

"I was trying to get my message across," she told him and then he pulled his fingers from her ass and replaced them with his cock. He pushed right in.

"The teddy would have done it, but the vibrator lets me know that you're up for anything."

She felt a bit of fear, and then Slayer was on one side and Cobra on the other side. "Get her arms," Turbo told them and Ford pulled her arms gently behind her back as Slayer and Cobra leaned down and began to suckle and pull on her nipples at the same time.

She cried out her release and moaned and bucked on top of Max.

"It's going to be one hell of a night indeed. Let's do her Special Forces style," Turbo said. She tightened up and then felt her body release more cream as all the men joined in together, loving her, possessing her, claiming her. Her breath caught in her throat, and she cried out another release and wondered how she would ever repay Precious back.

God Bless Special Forces!

THE END

WWW.DIXIELYNNDWYER.COM

Siren Publishing, Inc.
www.SirenPublishing.com

Lightning Source UK Ltd.
Milton Keynes UK
UKOW01f2311250817
307997UK00009B/437/P